somewhere in a desert

War has begun. No one knows where or how, but it has begun. Mouth open, it stands behind you, whispering. When it is over, no one will remain standing. No one will be spared.

J.M.G. Le Clézio, *War*

somewhere in a desert

dominique sigaud

arcade publishing • new york

FIRST U.S. EDITION

Originally published in French under the title *L'Hypothèse du désert* by
Editions Gallimard

The characters and events in this book are fictitious. Any similarity to
real persons, living or dead, is coincidental and not intended by the
author.

Library of Congress Cataloging-in-Publication Data
Sigaud, Dominique, 1959–
    [Hypothèse du désert. English]
    Somewhere in a desert / by Dominique Sigaud ; translated from
the French by Frank Wynne.
        p.   cm.
    ISBN 1-55970-492-6
    I. Wynne, Frank.   II.   Title.
PQ2679.I3375H9613   1999
843'.914—dc21   99-35306

Published in the United States by Arcade Publishing, Inc., New York
Distributed by Time Warner Trade Publishing

10 9 8 7 6 5 4 3 2 1

BP

PRINTED IN THE UNITED STATES OF AMERICA

part one

1

the defeated (i)

They sit in the shadows of their burned-out tanks, others stand or lie on the sand. They stare into the sun, they look at nothing else, or at nothing at all.

Their hair is white now. They don't speak to one another. They think about going home; all through the war they have thought of nothing else.

The young pace up and down, expressionless; they cannot bring themselves to look at the old soldiers, at these men who could be their fathers, for fear of the resignation, of the disgust they may find in their eyes.

They are nowhere. Here, they know no one can see; no one gives them a second thought. Here, they have ceased to exist, except perhaps in the memories of their families and their neighbours. No one gave them a second thought before the war, but back then, in their homes, roaming their streets, no more happy, no more afraid than the next man, it didn't matter. Only the hope that somewhere, strangers are thinking of them, might save them, but they know hope is futile. This is one of the things that war has taught them. Some of them believe it will kill them.

They think of the miles they would have to retrace. The sun again, and the dust, and the tiredness. The nights cold and too short, and the orders. Some are parched with thirst, but they have little water or food.

Night falls, and they think of those who deserted when the planes first showered them with leaflets telling them to surrender. They don't know where these men are now. The leaflets said they had nothing to fear. Some say that once captured, the men were tortured, but no one knows for certain.

They didn't want to die any more, they said, and they deserted; thousands of them with a single thought. The older men counted the sons they had lost in the last war and wondered why their deaths should be added to those of their children. Others wondered why they should die when their deaths would mean nothing? All they had were the days they had left until the end came. It would be enough to watch the vines creep round their houses and to wait for death when it would come.

They know that even if their lives are worthless it would be dishonourable to surrender. But they say this is a war without honour, a war of lies. They have been offered up. They have been chosen to die, that was why they were here: thousands of them already rotting in the sand.

When the war started they were given orders to advance into the desert. Within shelling distance of the border they stopped, dug their trenches and waited. Days on end.

After a while, they had to ration food; they would sit or stand motionless for hours, moving about only at night. There were too many nights, too much waiting; they began to think about the vines creeping round the houses, of the smell of sweet onions; they became bored and frightened. Only the thought of victory kept them strong, but it became impossible to imagine and the fear grew.

They watched the sky overhead. Somehow, it seemed to darken with each day, and since sleep would not come they began to speak in low voices.

They started to talk about their streets, about their children, about the peace there had been before; later they talked of fear and death. Their talk galvanised them, and one by one they resolved that they would not die here. It was then, finally, that the attack came. They were defeated, decimated.

2

somewhere in a desert (i)

The war was over. In the middle of the desert a man lay dead.

On the other side of the border were the defeated, their bodies torn apart, or strangely untouched, eyes closed, or open staring into the infinite, stiff hands gripping the earth. There were no women among them, the women had died elsewhere – in the villages or nearby; there were no children. Nothing but the bodies of soldiers – some young, barely in their teens, others older – and the acrid stench of rotting flesh. The dead seemed to stretch like a carpet over the sand.

The sun had begun to work on their skin, bloating, burning, twisting it, as the flesh flushed livid purple, then seemed to melt. The heavy cloth of their uniforms was more resistant. One day, the only sign of where they had fallen would be strips of material fluttering like bandages and scraps of flesh among the white young bones.

No camera crew came to film the bodies; it was as though they had never existed. Their killers were the first to forget them. Maybe at dusk some young soldier's memory would trick him and he would recollect the long, humid nights, waiting for war, and the others – less than a dozen – while it raged.

Only their families remembered; waited for them to come home and thought of them long afterwards, engulfed in a tomb of sand. But no one came to film them either.

Arms outstretched, the body of the man was turned towards the sun. He seemed more asleep than dead: his lips fixed in a half-smile, his eyes sometimes glittering in the sun and seeming to bring his face to life, though he had been lying here for days.

The border was on the far side of the dunes, several kilometres away. Where his body lay, the foreign troops had barely rumbled past. He himself was a foreigner. A soldier.

Nothing surrounded the body, nothing but the sand stretching to the north and south, sparse tufts of yellowed grass and the sun, red on the sands like an open wound. It was a desolate place, empty and slow, that could crush any living thing. But this man was dead now and at peace.

It was Ali ben Fakr who found him by accident, four days after the war ended. For the first time since war broke out, since peace returned, he had woken that morning to find the sky brighter; and so he didn't go to open his shop – a haberdashery, chemist and drapers on the main street of the village – instead he headed towards the stone bridge which marked the end of the village and, from there, took the path across the dunes. The path led nowhere, it simply linked a scattering of oil wells and some illegal trading posts which traded car tyres, jerry-cans, tools and, recently, helmets and military jackets.

This was the first time in months Ali ben Fakr had set foot into the desert. Though war had been fought on the other side of the border, off to the east, while foreign troops drove their armoured cars near the village or through the streets, he stayed at home.

The weather was pleasant: bright, not too hot, nor too cold, not a shadow crossed the sky. Now and then he stopped to feel the sun on his skin and felt himself come alive here in this place that he loved more than anything. His lungs swelled. Here, he found peace. Things were as they should be; war was no more than a distant memory – it might never have happened at all.

He left the path and cut quickly across the dunes; his feet were familiar with every hill and hollow. He knew the way the wind shifted them in the night. At this rate he would be at Faycal Mahdi's house in less than an hour. As he walked, he rehearsed his lines. He wouldn't say anything at first. Let Faycal go on and on about his new toys: the women, the jewels, the horses; then they would go to the stables. They would talk about the races, admire the mares, stroke their hindquarters and their hocks like thoroughbred breeders, then walk back to the fortress Mahdi was building in the desert. Ali ben Fakr would wait until they got to the door, then say, 'I want to buy Djamel.' Faycal would look at him and laugh, but before he had time to say, 'You're crazy! Do you know how much she's worth?' Ali would take out his money. He wanted the thoroughbred bay. It would cost him everything he had, everything he had saved over twenty years, but what matter? It was what he wanted.

The village had long since disappeared behind him; the dead soldier lay only yards ahead, but Ali ben Fakr passed close by without seeing him. He was half-way up the next dune when he stopped and turned, even then barely a shrug, thinking he had seen a dead dog or maybe a horse. To catch Faycal Mahdi he would have to get there before eleven; if he hurried he could be there early. Faycal Mahdi liked people to be early. 'The old bastard,' he muttered, thinking of his friend's stubby fingers glittering with signet rings – he was rich now they had found oil on his land – his permanently half-closed eyes. If he didn't want this horse, didn't need it like a baby needs the breast, he would keep him waiting all day. 'Old bastard,' he muttered again, not knowing why. He stopped, thinking about the body he had just passed, and turned. He could barely make it out. He walked back a few steps and stopped: it was not a dog, but a man, lying here in the middle of nowhere. The dead man, his body turned towards the sun.

Ali ben Fakr was reluctant to go to him. He thought about the thoroughbred in his stable, about the desert, calm and peaceful around him, the wad of crumpled notes in his pocket. He had only a couple of miles to go to Faycal Mahdi's place. But the man might still be alive; so he took a few steps towards the body, stopping dead when he recognised the man's fatigues and army boots.

Sweat trickled on his forehead. The war – a brief parenthesis –

was over. Why should this soldier be his concern; why, when there was no one around to see? He took a step forward, then back, walked away and stopped, cursed, his hands sweaty, his forehead slick. Then he made his decision: alive, I take care of him; dead, I leave him and he walked towards the body again. The man's eyes were wide, stared fixedly at the sky, his limp body lay on the sand and Ali ben Fakr looked away. He shook his sandals, careful not to look down at the corpse. He shrugged off any nagging qualm of conscience and turned to leave. He had wasted enough time; in any case, there was nothing he could do for this man. He was probably a foreign soldier who had got lost.

He started on, feeling hot now, thinking about the horse, but at the top of the dune, inexplicably, he turned back. The corpse lay below, bathed in the sunlight, 'lost to everyone,' Ali ben Fakr thought. He kept walking, but more slowly now. The sun pounded his temples and suddenly, for no reason, he felt weak. Perhaps he was just tired and hot, maybe he had set out too early. Possibly it was the body, lying on its back like some shop-window dummy sunbathing. But there was nothing he could do. It was bad enough that this man had come here, he and thousands like him, slashing through the silence. The sand would take his body, closing over him, and the wound in the desert would heal without a scar, all would be as it should be.

Ali ben Fakr could feel his pulse beat irregularly and couldn't stop himself from turning again towards the silhou- ette, supine, far below. He looked at this piece of human meat and felt his heart squeezed by a fist. For a moment he thought, 'I could be lying there in his place.' He took his bag, set it in the sand and sat down; he couldn't know that he was doing precisely what the man had done in that very spot, some days before, caught by the same sudden flush of tiredness.

The shadow of the soldier shivered in the heat haze, his palms turned upward towards the sky. Ali ben Fakr looked at his own hands, feeling more alone than he had ever been; he brought his hands to his face, turned to the man and stared at him. It was then, without knowing why, that he rose to cross the short distance that separated them.

When he got to the soldier, Ali ben Fakr bowed mechanically and prayed to God; the man was smiling. A moment ago he might have been laughing. There was a peaceful glimmer in his eyes and, strangely, not a mark on his body. Ali ben Fakr crouched beside this man who had been lying dead for days, or perhaps for only an hour, and smiling still as though in an instant he would get up. For a moment he felt at peace.

The desert stretched out around them, infinite, with not a shadow nor a sound; the sand showed no signs of the foreign troops that had passed through, nothing but the body of this soldier. This man that he had never seen before, buttoned up tight in his army fatigues, arms thrown out on the sand, dead and at peace, so Ali ben Fakr stretched out his hand to close the man's eyes. It was a reflex, the gesture of the living to the dead, a sign to send the man into eternity; a way of drawing a line between the war and the peace. But his hand stopped before he could do it. He knew nothing of this man, of the bodies which had given life to him or those which had held him, caressed him, hurt him. He did not know why the man was lying here, smiling, when the war was over. Closing the man's eyes would cut him off for ever from the world where he still lay, peacefully; it would be like killing him. All the same, he should do it; he couldn't leave the body staring distractedly out into the world. It had to be done, the difference between them had to be marked.

Ali ben Fakr tried a second time and failed. Later, he thought, he would do it later, when he had spent some time with this man, time enough to cut him off from everything without regret. Then he thought that he would have to bury the man, too. It was, he knew, his responsibility, not only for the soldier's sake, to set him at rest in the quiet earth, but for himself, so that everything was in order again. But if he did this, he would be the last one to bend over this man, the last person in his life, his final witness. He knew that if he buried this man the memory would be with him always, and he wondered whether he was prepared to have the chalkmark of this life on his own. If he were thirty, perhaps, like the soldier, he might have thought that he was simply burying a dead soldier. But at his age, how could he bury this man without feeling that he was being buried alongside him? In putting him in the ground, this man he did not know – this stranger who meant nothing to him, to whom he meant nothing – making him vanish from the world, he felt that he too would somehow disappear. It was then he realised he would not do it.

Ali ben Fakr covered his face with his hands. It looked as though he was crying, but he did not cry. Sweat began to trickle again on his forehead; he drank some water but his throat dried at once. He felt his head spin and he fell, unconscious, by the soldier's body.

Nothing moved except the sun, arcing across the two men. No one could tell what thoughts fermented behind the closed eyes of the one, nor the wide stare of the other, but from time to time Ali ben Fakr's face twitched involuntarily as tension seeped from his muscles, as tiredness ebbed.

He was woken a little later by the shadow of a vulture, high in the sky. The sun beat down on him, directly above, he felt his heart beat erratically. He looked at the man beside him, the smooth, childish face, the mouth a bitter crease, and for a moment he couldn't tell if he had ever seen him before, if he had known him all his life, or if this face, still unmarked by death, was a reflection of his own. For a second he forgot the war was over and thought he must be dying here, bleeding into the sand. Perhaps he had killed this man, unless the man had killed him. He felt a scream rise in him, then he saw the dunes and remembered where he was and why.

He looked at his watch and realised it was too late now to go to Faycal Mahdi. His legs felt heavy. He pushed himself off the sand and stood, once again face to face with the dead man. He wanted to shout at him to wake up. He put his ear to the man's lips but they were cold, the mouth open on nothingness, no whisper of breath. Ali ben Fakr got up and suddenly he could see himself here on the dune, alone and growing old; his penis hung lifeless between his fat, heavy thighs, his fingers were as short and stubby as Faycal Mahdi's, his belly folded over itself and spilled on to his groin. He saw all this in a moment and he let his eyes fall. Death seemed closer to him than to this young soldier and he felt fear tighten round him suddenly, a fear so vast that it would have swallowed him whole if the image of the thoroughbred bay had not flickered, like a dream, through his mind. The animal moving over the sand like a leopard hunting, racing against his peers. Brushing against the leaders to put them off, pulling back only when it could feel the tension and then, in the final lengths, alone and proud, his mane up, the sand whipping around him as though nothing and no one could ever stop him. For this horse Ali ben Fakr had counted five hundred notes into his bag each of a thousand. Over and over he counted them, counting all his days and rolling them into this fat wad held fast by a worn elastic band. He wore it close to him, next to his skin. The money was twenty years of his life. Twenty years for a thoroughbred he couldn't even ride. Beside him on the sand the corpse seemed to laugh – in his place, Ali would have done the same.

The palms of the body were turned upwards towards heaven, as though reaching out or holding on, but there was nothing around him. And his smile . . . why did he not scream; dying out here like a mongrel? What had happened to shut off his life like this? What were his last words, his last thoughts? Why would a soldier, in civilian dress, lie down to die here, unarmed, in the shadow of the dune. Did he know that had he walked another hour he would have been in Rijna?

Ali ben Fakr's throat tightened again; he stood and looked up at the sky. He had to go, he had to leave now before it drove him mad.

Half-way up the dune he turned one last time; the man lay in the hollow, bathed in sunlight, he could hardly tear his eyes away.

*

When he got back to Rijna, Ali ben Fakr went directly to the market square. It was a little before one o'clock. As on every Tuesday and Thursday, the market was bustling. Men were testing the soft flesh of the fat, juicy melons laid out on blankets spread on the sand or in the shadow of the arches, but Ali ben Fakr went straight to the men sitting in the café.

He was sweating and one of the men laughed and asked him what was wrong. Someone shouted: 'Wife got you running round after her again?' But he simply mumbled something like you won't believe this and, without waiting to draw breath, told them of what he had found in the desert and the men – usually so talkative – fell silent as mouthing carp.

They had never seen Ali ben Fakr in such a state. They knew he was a genius for spinning stories, he could sell you the wind. There wasn't one of them who hadn't bought enough pots and pans and fake gold pens from him to last them for three generations. They had never heard him speak like this. His eyes cast down, no wild gesticulations, even in his voice there seemed to be something missing. They didn't dare look at him. They didn't even think to ask what the man looked like, what uniform he was wearing, whether he was dark-haired or blond, whether he had a moustache, whether he was armed.

The fresh memories of war sprang up; the howling of planes hunting at night high above them, and further off, in the dunes, the deadened thump of heavy artillery. They remembered their sour dreams, the wondering in the night if this was the end. Remembered staring at their hands as though even their own movements eluded them. And then the foreign troops marching through the village, the soldiers too blond, their voices too loud and nasal. The way they spoke to the villagers without ever looking at them and drank from their flasks though there was plenty of water in the village. Hardly had they got out of their jeeps when they were demanding telephones. It was the only time they ever spoke. Some offered cigarettes or chewing gum, as though they thought the villagers had never seen cigarettes or chewing gum before. It made the children laugh, and they would say 'thank you, thank you' in English and the soldiers would take photos of them. Then they got back in their trucks and were never seen again. In the beginning, they thought it was funny. Some of them said, 'How would they like it if we went driving through their towns saying "Stand back, stand back" and talking about bringing order and peace and never drank a drop of their water?' But even they stopped talking and acted as though the war had never happened. Only during their games of dominos were they more silent. Without noticing, they began to go home early, to let their conversations trail off. In the end, some of them said the armies of infidels had desecrated the land of their fathers, but they knew it was just words, it didn't mean anything.

It was the war they thought about, as they listened to Ali ben Fakr talking about the soldier in fatigues laid out on the sand, a war they hadn't started, which they could feel again, a heavy weight on each of them, and so they fell silent. In the market-place the men were closing up. They drifted towards the café and, finding their friends there, mute as headstones, asked them what was wrong.

Ali Ben Fakr told his story again, then once more to those who came later. Soon there were thirty of them around the table. News scurried around the market square and into the side streets. Some older men who had stayed silent began to ask questions. Where was this man? Another asked who he was, a third what he was wearing and a fourth the colour of his hair. Suddenly there were a score of voices together and Ali Ben Fakr let them talk, then he shouted at them to shut up and asked them if they were sure that none of them had seen anything unusual in the dunes recently. Could each of them swear they hadn't seen a body, maybe far off? The men rifled through their memories. They couldn't really remember. Maybe, now he mentioned it, they had seen something. Maybe they'd even stopped for a minute without really knowing why. But not one of them went near; they walked away.

'What's happened to us?' enquired Ali ben Fakr then and they said nothing; 'what sort of men have we become?' he asked again, but no one answered. Only the blind man's son spoke up and said that they should bury the man before the dogs ate him, but Ali ben Fakr didn't want to go back to the dunes so soon. Later, he suggested, when it was cooler – and he went home.

As soon as he got in, Nour wanted to know where he had been. Why had he been up so early? Had he gone to see Faycal Mahdi about the horse. She knew all about his plans, he had talked about them often enough. 'You went to see him,' she said, 'and he wouldn't sell you the horse? He wouldn't sell, would he?' but he didn't answer. He got up from the table and went to his room, and when she came in he turned towards the wall and pretended to sleep.

He couldn't get the image of the dead soldier out of his mind. He wondered if someone had left the body there deliberately, thinking no one would find it, or maybe because they knew that one day it would be found. But who? and why? Why else would this man be lying there alone in such a place?

He closed his eyes and thought about the dunes, and the silhouette of the lifeless body below, and his fear. The man was still there, arms flung wide in the sun's glare. He had run away. How could he have run away from the unmarked body of this young soldier? As he fell asleep he felt the urge to go back there. In his dreams he saw a face turned into the shadows and heard a river of words coming from the man, but he couldn't understand them and it was this which woke him. The bed beside him was empty. He got up, then, and went out.

He went to his shop and opened it, but he left the metal grille half closed. He served two or three customers who happened to be passing. The blind man's son came by late in the afternoon and suggested that they go and bury the soldier now, while they had two or three hours before twilight, but Ali ben Fakr said that they would go tomorrow, at dawn, when it was cool. Then, a little before sunset, he closed up the shop and headed off alone towards the dunes.

The mound of stones he had left on the near side of the dune was easily found and, from there, the place itself. He walked the last few yards slowly, shocked again by the silhouette lying on the sand in the last of the daylight. The man's arms were stretched out as though he were laughing and his eyes seemed to be fixed on something far off, beyond the horizon; for a second he was surprised to find that no sand had drifted on to his clothes or his open palms. He thought that something about the man had changed, but he couldn't tell what. Maybe the wind had simply resculpted the dune around him.

He sat near the body. The impending dark crept over the surrounding dunes, the sand, soft as linen, was cool in his fingers, the man was smiling still. Ali ben Fakr looked at the young man's face. It was peaceful and gentle; this was the face of a man who loved, a man who was gentle and loving. For no reason it reminded Ali ben Fakr of himself as a young man, when he had believed he would spend his whole life travelling and selling his earthenware. He could see his entire life stretching out, with no regrets and no defeat. He was twenty then, and now twenty seemed so young, so far away and all he had left of it was this vague memory. Even then, he was probably learning how to lie, and how to be silent. But he had fought too, in his own way: a gang of them would meet at night and talk about human rights, talk about the rights that no one mentioned in daylight. They loved the secrecy of the meetings and they loved to lie. It was nearly forty years ago. He had never thought about it since; now, looking at the dead soldier, he knew why. One image rose up from this heap of old memories. Faroud, lying dead in the desert, a bullet in his head.

Ali ben Fakr looked down, dropped his head, his whole body and disappeared. He was the one who had found Faroud, by accident, a couple of kilometres outside the village. Here was no stranger, they had been born a street apart. It was Faroud who organised the meetings and Faroud who had persuaded Ali ben Fakr to come to them. He was ten years older than the rest of them and his talk was wild and full of metaphors. They called him the poet. He said they had to do justice to their country's future, bring it alive, make it love, words like that; it lasted three months. They never knew which of them had turned him in. When they had shot him, the authorities left his body in the desert so the others would say nothing. And they said nothing; they never met together again.

For a second, the soldier's face looked to Ali ben Fakr like the poet's face; last night he had run away from the second as thirty years ago he had run from the first, and the days that followed simply helped him to forget; now, they were weightless in his life, no more than a hoof print on sand taken by the breeze. That's what death is, he thought, something like that, a life become weightless, taken by the breeze, and he thanked heaven that the dead soldier was here before him, otherwise he would have gone mad.

It was dark and Ali ben Fakr remembered that they were to bury the soldier the next day. He leaned over the body again, looked into the beautiful face and he suddenly felt an immense sadness. He felt he wanted to start over, be another man, to throw down his life and live again, say things unsaid and move again, fall silent again, give up, remember and then he turned to the dead soldier and asked: 'Who would forgive me if I did,' but the soldier didn't answer. His face was in darkness now, he seemed far off, caught up in old memories, and for the second time that day Ali ben Fakr felt more alone than he had ever been.

He wanted to spend the night here, beside the body, and

remember everything that he had done, but he didn't want to get back too late to face Nour's questions. He decided to go. He had the whole night to think about what he had done with his life, and what he might do with it now. It was terrifying. Nour's body beside him seemed alien, the house seemed alien, all around, the sleeping sky, the palm trees and the earth seemed strangers; everything was turning from him, slipping through his fingers. He waited for day to follow night, and at dawn the blind man's son came with three others and knocked at his door. They had brought spades and for a moment Ali ben Fakr thought they had come to bury him.

The four men crossed the deserted village in the chill dawn air. Around them the dunes slowly paled; from time to time one of their sandals would kick up a relic from the troops who had passed, a shard of metal or a piece of a blown tyre, and bury it with its heel. When they got to the dune and saw the body, the men with Ali ben Fakr stopped and the war came back to them in a torrent. Only the blind man's son smiled, but Ali ben Fakr didn't know why.

Later, the youngest of them noticed that the man wasn't wearing a military dog tag, he said only a doctor could tell exactly when he died, but they had gone back with their armies; besides, they realised that it was pointless to try and find out. Their spades lay on the sand. Perhaps they should wait a while before burying him, one suggested, someone might recognise him; his face was unmarked and perfectly preserved. After all, he said, there's no hurry. Ali ben Fakr smiled, but the blind man's son shouted something like 'Have you forgotten the law? God's law says we must bury his sons, whoever they are, as soon as possible.' They hadn't forgotten, they knew that the law said a burial should take place within twenty-four hours. But this was not their death and didn't God's law say that a man should be buried with his name? It didn't matter anyway. The blind man's son stood waiting, his face sweating with rage as he waited, but no one answered. They knew him and since his father had died they were used to hearing him spit venom. Ali ben Fakr said simply that they would decide when they got back to the village and they left.

A crowd of men were waiting for them at the café. They explained what they had seen and why they had not buried the soldier. Someone said the only thing to do was for all of them to go there and deal with the body.

When the sun had gone down a little, twenty men set off and headed for the dune. There were no women, of course. No father, husband or son, not the gentle, nor the braggarts, nor the most loving had spoken about this to them. Most of them hadn't even thought of it.

Ali ben Fakr said that they should put stones around the body so that the sand, churned up by their feet, would not take it. Then he sat and watched.

Farouk el-Bassan was the first to go to the body, but he turned away quickly, his stomach sick. He had been the village butcher for more than twenty years, they knew him to be as good-natured as he was a coward and he had celebrated the end of the war like a condemned man his pardon. A dozen lambs were roasted on a fire in his garden, and he sang and danced in a party that lasted for four days and nights. The next morning he had painted all the doors and shutters in his house in bright, raucous colours, and he sat out on his freshly painted doorstep and stopped passers-by with the same pleasantries he always had. War had reminded him forcefully of the frailty of life. From the moment war broke out, the ground in his dreams gave way underfoot, and the path was pitted with holes and crevices. He had spent his waking hours trying to convince himself of man's immortality and, specifically, his own. He walked away from the body and tried to forget he had seen it; no one attempted to stop him.

An old man turned towards Ali ben Fakr, who had seen him often, sitting on the banks of the dry riverbed, and enquired when the soldier had died. Ali ben Fakr knew the man was asking how much longer he would live and gave no answer.

The other men looked at the soldier, their eyes glazed. No one spoke. They knew the moment they saw his sandy skin and his clothes – the same ordinary fatigues they had all seen or worn many times – that they would never know in which army he had served. Their spit and their jibes stuck in their throats; here was simply a dead man among the dead, another corpse in the carnage, a soul freed of its shell, they thought, a thing inert, a thing they would become in their turn. His eyes seemed alive, now dark and shadowy, now glittering and luminous, as the sun arced overhead. Some saw them open on to a great truth. . . . The track like a wrinkle, of a long dry tear under one eye, seemed printed on his face like a sign of mourning, a last thought, a last regret, a final hesitation before quitting his body, and seeing it, the men could not but be touched with compassion for the man. Around his body the desert seemed to hush; the roaring memories of bombers, of soldiers in their tanks had seeped away, the sirens, and the screams they sometimes heard still, in the evenings, if they listened hard. There was nothing here but the whisper of their feet on the sand, the rustle of the air in the heat; everyday murmurings, and the men began to speak quietly for the simple pleasure of hearing the forgotten tones of their voices. Ali ben Fakr watched those who had been with him at the poet's meetings. Sweat beaded on their foreheads, their arms fell limp by their sides; he knew that they too remembered the day and he waited.

The body was still not buried when the sky began to darken. None of them had the courage to do it; later, they said, they would do it tomorrow. They would come back and bury him; then, in groups, they left. When they came to the hill above the village they saw the last of the daylight had painted the walls sepia and ochre. Eyman ibn Sa'abi turned then, and went to Ali ben Fakr.

The two men had been born on the same May morning, only an hour apart; they had grown up like twins, like brothers; everything they did, everything they learned, they did together. The day he turned eighteen, Ali ben Fakr married Eyman's younger sister, who died giving birth a few years later, and then there was the poet. No one suspected that the two went to all the meetings together – everyone thought they were at Al Majnoun's cattle mart, or out gambling at the races.

Over the years, as Ali ben Fakr grew expansive and fat, Eyman ibn Sa'abi became dry and taciturn. Little by little he had climbed the hierarchy of the local mosque, respected almost as a *cadi* for his thin-lipped austerity and feared for his network of connections with the great and the good. At first the men stopped meeting as a precaution, later they did so through habit; in the end they avoided each other, and when Ali ben Fakr would launch into one of his thunderous sermons in the café – about the severity of taxes or the stupidity of a local magistrate – his old friend would turn on his heels and mutter, 'When he got fat, it wasn't just from the neck down.'

Even the war didn't bring them together. Ali ben Fakr complained long and loud about it, while Eyman tried to convince his countrymen of the righteousness of a war that would bring peace and justice back to them. This was the first time they had seen each other since the war.

Eyman walked in silence alongside Ali ben Fakr, until the latter finally spoke: 'I thought about the poet yesterday; I hadn't thought about him for thirty-five years.'

'Not a day goes by that I don't think about him,' replied Eyman. 'Not a single day.'

The two men spent the night talking and by dawn had told all that had happened to them in thirty-five years. When Ali ben Fakr woke the following morning he realised that this was the first time he had spoken about the poet since his death. The following day they were joined by another friend from the old days, then another. In the evening, coming back from the dune, they walked along the dry riverbed and talked, wondering aloud if, now that they were older, they might dare to speak of rights and of power. Ali ben Fakr was smiling broadly. He didn't know that for the fourth night in a row his wife, Nour al-Koutoubi, lay unable to sleep, staring into the dark.

Nour al-Koutoubi was seventeen when she married. They had always known each other; she was the eldest niece of the father of Ali ben Fakr's first wife and so had the luxury of watching him from afar long before he ever spoke to her. She had seen his hair grow grey and his belly fat; she had heard his thunderous laugh and his lightning temper. Later, after his first wife died, she felt his gaze drawn to her, grazing the nape of her neck, her breasts, sliding down to her hips to stop at the mound between her legs.

When she was told he had asked for her hand in marriage she laughed. No one knew if she was laughing at his proposal or if she was happily accepting; she simply laughed, then went to speak to one of her aunts, long widowed. Some hours later she left her aunt, knowing more about marriage than many twice her age. Not long afterwards she said yes. It was Nejma who explained to her how to make the best use of siestas and, once married, she did just that, until the war came.

Of the war she had seen nothing but a couple of tanks rolling through the village, heard the muffled sound of the battle beyond the dunes and, though she was curious to see the soldiers in their white shorts walking around the streets of Rijna, she instinctively kept her distance. She knew little of the reasons for all this trouble; once or twice, in the long evenings, Ali ben Fakr would say something about the weak and the power of the strong, but she didn't try to find out more. When she caught angry snatches of conversation between the men in the street, saying: 'They think they can do what they like,' she didn't try to find out who 'they' were. The only difference was that she was careful not to let the children stray beyond the palm groves and if she learned to laugh a little less, she did so without noticing.

When Ali ben Fakr told her one morning that the war was over she was happy. She pulled him to her and they made love, then she set about washing all the bed linen and the towels, the table-cloths, the curtains. The next day, when he talked about the thoroughbred bay again, she said nothing. He had talked about it since the first time she met him. On his return from the dunes, silent and gloomy, she was sure that Faycal Mahdi had refused his offer. But that night he came home later than usual, and when she woke in the morning she found the place beside her empty and began to wonder if there was another woman.

She would watch him as he left, expecting to see the nervous step, almost a dance, of men anxious to get back to a body that is new and barely explored; but no, his step was still heavy and slow and, two days later, he made love to her again. This time it was different; he held back his orgasm, though she knew he was not usually patient. He moved inside her as though he was trying to tell her something, something wordless. She began to notice other changes: a different resonance in his voice, a wistful nostalgia in the way he looked, even his gait seemed to change – it was as though he were somewhere else, or walking backwards; and so, one night, she decided to find out what was going on, and when he got up at dawn and went out she followed him.

She followed him as he crossed the stone bridge, along the path, then from dune to dune, stopping when he stopped, holding her breath when he was downwind and crouching in the sand when she felt he might turn round, until she saw him stop on the spill of a dune; there were others there, men, she knew every one.

Lying out of sight on the sand, she observed them for a time and understood that they were standing around a body. She watched them until the sight almost blinded her, but nothing happened. No one moved, no one seemed to speak. She turned and went back, and spent the day wondering what madness had got into them all. Whose body was stretched on the sand and why did they stand around it, why did they not bury it? But when Ali ben Fakr came home late in the night she asked no questions. She waited until he was asleep, then got up, took her darkest shawls and went out. The village streets were deserted by the dogs themselves. When she saw the desert ahead, a black, bottomless pit, Nour al-Koutoubi pulled her shawls tighter about her. For a moment she felt more alone than she had ever felt; then, trembling, she started out across the dunes. The footprints of the men had been obliterated. She thought she heard something and turned back, but nothing moved, the desert was silent and black, the stars barely shining.

An hour later she came to the dune where she had seen her husband stop. The body lay a little below. She held her breath when she first saw it and again when she came within yards of it. She was afraid, it was madness to have come here, and she thought about turning back. If she stayed much longer she might not find her way back, but just as she was about to turn and go, the moon came out and the sand was flooded with a soft white light, and Nour al-Koutoubi realised that the place where she stood was bathed in a slow calm, and so she walked forward, her fingers clenched tightly against her palms, until she came to the man. She leaned over him. He seemed to be asleep. His hands lay on the sand, his hair fell in curls on his forehead, he looked beautiful, she thought. She sat down. The gentleness of his features, like a mask over his face, shone in the white brilliance of the moon. He was young, smiling. She had never seen death close up before. She knew the strange calm of the corpse must have affected the village men and began to understand why Ali ben Fakr had been so different of late.

After a while, her legs numbed with sleep, she stood, head thrown back, and looked into the coal-black dome of the sky. She wondered if this man had been in the tanks rumbling through the desert, one of the sunburned soldiers in the light shorts. She thought she heard a laugh from behind her and turned, but it was only a dog howling, then she felt the sand shift slightly under her feet and, instinctively, she moved towards the corpse; his head was turned and he was staring at her.

Nour al-Koutoubi steps back. She turns and looks away, far away; far beyond the dunes which, all around, stretch out as far as the eye can see, farther than the vastness of night and the sky; she is looking for something, some fixed point, something to remind her of the order of things: that life and death are separate and distinct and she can never know the ties that bind them. She feels a terrifying loneliness, the earth seems to shift, she wants to cry, to scream, the gates of hell slam shut behind her; her face and hands already disintegrating; she falls to her knees, blinded by the darkness, she crumples and the man beside her speaks: 'Don't be afraid.'

She doesn't want to hear. She stops her ears. She says – she screams – that she didn't hear anything, but her fear strikes no fear in the man and he says the words once more. She stands up again, but the sand shifts from beneath her, her knees bend, she feels she is going to die; for a second, she wants to die. She looks up and sees the sky, black and empty, only then does she dare look down at the man.

Gently, he says again, 'Don't be afraid.' He knows this woman will not break so easily.

But she turns away, certain she is going mad. 'I have to go,' she says, 'I have to go back, go back, I have to leave now.' She tries to get up but her legs refuse to work, she feels her mouth open and a voice she doesn't recognise says simply: 'But you're dead.'

The man seems to smile, he closes his eyes. 'You're right, I am dead,' he says. She doesn't find it funny. She stands and pulls her shawls about her and just as she sets off she hears him ask, 'Will you come back?'

She was still shaking from head to foot when she got home. She slipped into bed beside Ali ben Fakr, pressed herself against his body and kissed him. He didn't open his eyes but rolled over on to her and slipped inside her. Afterwards she cried for a long time. She didn't know if it was the familiar pleasure that made her cry, or the words she had heard from a man she was certain was dead.

When she woke, she went to see her aunt, Nejma. The old woman, ensconced in her chair, made Nour al-Koutoubi tell the story in detail three times, her walking stick hovering as she listened. She sat quietly for a long time, a smile playing on her lips, and when she finally woke from her dream she looked at her niece, smiled and said: 'If I didn't know you, child, I'd think you'd lost your head and pray to Allah for your mother's soul. But I know you well, and if my old legs would carry me I'd go with you to where you saw this body. Go back, take two or three women you can trust with you and return there tonight. Maybe your mind was playing tricks on you and then again, maybe not . . . God go with you.'

Later, Nour went to see her closest friends. Their husbands had stood around the corpse the night before. So as not to frighten them, she started by telling them of how Ali ben Fakr had changed and, as she expected, the three women confessed that their husbands were behaving strangely too. Nour told them how she had wondered if Ali ben Fakr had been unfaithful, how she had followed him to the dune and what she had seen there: their husbands, the body. She told them what had happened afterwards, how she had gone into the desert at night, how the dead man had turned to her, what he had said. Then she told them about her visit to Nejma.

The women listened in silence; each of them wondering if Nour al-Koutoubi had gone out of her mind. But they had known her all their lives and they agreed to go with her into the desert.

As planned, the four women met just before midnight behind the stone bridge. The moon, shrouded in cloud, threw dark shadows, the path was deserted, they were afraid. This was the first time they had gone out like this, without telling anyone, but Nour al-Koutoubi was determined and they would follow her to the end.

When they got to the top of the dune Nour pointed to the corpse below. The women waited and let her go ahead alone, then they went and joined her. They stood motionless before the body of the soldier, their dark veils slapping in the wind, covering their faces.

For a long moment they waited. The man lay there, eyes closed, hands pressed against the earth. The women began to think that Nour al-Koutoubi had been dreaming; but then, as the night before, he turned and looked at her. His lips parted, the ink-black sky glistened overhead, the dunes were shrouded in silence and the man began to speak. He talked all night without stopping, though he never told them who he was. He talked about the war and the destruction, the horror of the final battles. He spoke of the soldiers, their fingers trembling on triggers, become suddenly precise and sure, of the ground shaking day and night, of the acrid smell of cannon-fire and the stench of fear; the retching terror and the convulsions that heaved the last shreds of peace from the soul. He talked of the shattered bodies of children and the bleeding women walking like ghosts in the rubble of their houses. He told them of enemy lines, of the battlefields, of the lines of deserters wiped out in a horror of blood and metal, of prisoners sobbing on their knees, of men crying out in their sleep, of gaunt men talking of those they have seen die in front of them. He spoke of the soldiers, tired and mute, those who wanted to get it all over and those who laughed loud in the face of death; hundreds of people speaking dozens of languages, the food, spicy or bland, fatty or frugal, bony shoulders rubbing up with stocky, but all shuddering when they felt a hand on them.

He let out a sob; he had seen women in the prime of life lying on bloody stretchers and others let down their hair and lift their skirts at night when the music started up in the barracks. He had seen a child soldiers had found in a makeshift shelter, the boy's foot had been torn off, he was shaking, he couldn't even remember his own name. He had drunk piss-weak coffee with silent men waiting for the war to start; he had walked with them through the night, listening to them talk about the war, so different from all the others. He had sensed their fear, their confusion, sometimes their hatred. When he said the word, he lowered his eyes and his voice dropped to a whisper: he had seen men kill each other without so much as a look, and others pleading for life even as it drained out of them. He had heard their screams . . . He didn't finish the sentence; he gestured with his hand, as though hitting the air, closed his eyes and said no more. The women saw the long furrow across his brow, as though he were crying, and came closer to him. Silence; none of them dared move, the words he had spoken churned inside them like ashes. Then, in a muffled voice, the eldest of the women begged forgiveness and absolution – but for whom? The soldier heard and turned towards her in silence, then closed his eyes again.

Day would break soon, it was time for the women to leave; the man knew this and asked: 'Will you come back?' but the women got up without replying. They walked back in silence and when they got to the village they separated. In the dunes, though they could not know, the man was smiling.

Later that day Nour al-Koutoubi went back to see her Aunt Nejma and told here everything that had happened that night. The old woman listened in silence until she had finished, her eyes glazed, then she stood, leaning heavily on her cane, and said simply: 'Blessed are those whom God has chosen to bear witness, for without them the world would be damned.'

The following night there were ten women on the dune, young and old, widowed, married and virgins, all sat in silence. Some wept when they saw the man, for he reminded them of old hurts, of love that was faded and lost. His silence reminded them of the interminable silence of their own men sometimes, reminded them too how they wished life could be different. A life without all the battles lost in the early hours, the vengeful words spat in the heat of the afternoon, with nothing more than the will to hurt in the foolish belief that this was love. Some were afraid of hearing the soldier speak, they wanted to give in before he had begun, for what would life be like living with the weight of his words? But they stayed. They had always wanted a man to speak to them; they wanted nothing else. That he was a stranger, that he was dead, mattered little.

He did not know of their questions or their doubts. He smiled at them. He heard Nour al-Koutoubi come to him, her voice low and full of pity, and he smiled. He felt her veils flutter against him, but though he had spent days and nights in the lonely grip of death, and though he ached to see her, he didn't move. He knew she had come in secret – he had heard the men say that the women should not know. But now they were here and death did not hurt him any more; the hands he wanted to stretch out to them lay on the sand, he never moved. Through the long nights only his voice, his words, moved over them.

Then, one night, he didn't talk of war, but of death. Not of the brutal separation, nor the pain and the terror; he didn't speak of the sordid end, of the tears or the regret, but of the after-death: the sudden feeling of space, a limitless space, rising before him like dawn breaking again at midday; of the dazzling glare in his heart; of the laughter bubbling out of all the laughter that fear had bottled up within him all his life; of the heady drunkenness of knowing everything and of the peace, infinite and expanding like the sun on midsummer day, lighting up the beauty and the ugliness that man is born to, which breaks him and from which he rises, screaming, and struggles to stand and go on, carried forward by the glare of his most secret thoughts and of the smiles that break over his face, magical and radiant, leaving no trace. He had seen the men of Rijna lean over him, their minds half-open, wanting to know but fearful of the ignorance they would have to give up. He had seen his own life, had cried over it; he had everything and yet he had lived like a miser, like a beggar, and later, when he had understood, when he realised what man was – half-god, half-dog – he laughed. He laughed for nights on end; lying here beneath the stars; he laughed, around him only the sand stretching on for ever. He laughed at who he was and who he might have been, at the fury and carnage of men. And then he cried once more: for their wounded, those who were so close, and for so little, but they had not an inkling of it. The women stood by, their hearts beating fit to burst; they weren't thinking of men or of children, they had forgotten their fear and their regrets and they came back from the desert changed; like the men.

On the eighth night the women knew this would be the last; the soldier's face had hardened and he stuttered and fumbled for words. He realised this too. He said all the things he had held back, his last fears, his final wishes, then he was silent.

At first, when they heard his voice again, far off, somehow empty, the women thought he was talking to God; but he was talking to them. He spoke to them, for the first time, of a woman. His hands sketched out the silhouette of a body he would never know again; his voice was white now, his face closed, he was not looking at them. He was eaten up by emptiness and the women, forgetting their modesty, caressed his forehead; one last loving gesture and they sang softly, sang him to sleep, sang to relieve his pain.

Dawn came. The soldier turned to Nour al-Koutoubi and gestured; something the others did not see. The women did not cry. The man asked that no ceremony be done for him. 'Death', he told them, 'is more than enough' and he turned away.

*

The following day the men came and found the soldier's body suddenly eaten away with putrefaction; smelling of sickness and death, and they buried him without stone or ceremony, not knowing where he was from.

3

the defeated (ii)

The child went out to get milk, as she did every morning. Coming home, dawdling, over the bridge, she swung the basket on the end of her arm. The air was soft with the coming spring. She hummed.

In the plane, the gunner saw the bridge, adjusted his sights and pressed the button, as the man beside him shouted 'fire'. The first shell fell on the bank behind the child, her body shook like a pane of glass and the bridge trembled and she saw the water glinting below her. For a second she thought about jumping, but she didn't know how to swim, so she ran. Behind her she could hear people shouting, she could make out the high-pitched voices of the old women, screaming like stuck pigs, but her father had told her: 'If there's trouble some day, and there's no place for you to shelter, run and keep running; don't turn back, no matter how much you want to.' And he had added, 'You always want to turn back when things like that happen.'

She hadn't reached the other bank when the second plane came. Her heart turned over in panic, her sandals had fallen off, but she looked up and ran faster, her chest thrust forward, arms away from her body. It was then that she saw the man on the other side. He was looking at her. Around him people ran around screaming in all directions, but he just stood there. He walked forward a little towards her.

When the first shell dropped he had seen her body shake and stopped dead. He heard the second plane coming. He thought he saw the child stop for a second, as if she were giving up. But she pushed off again with her heels and ran, leaning forward, her arms out in front of her, and he stared at her, willing her on with all his strength and started to shout.

The child felt the second plane coming like a burning sensation on her back. She stumbled for the first time and got up again without once taking her eyes off the man. Behind her the noise was louder, the plane was flying low; she stumbled again. As she did, she saw the man stretch out his arms towards her and scream, 'Run!' And so she got up again as best she could. Her ankle hurt. She could hear her heartbeat hammering in her head, she was scared, she was terribly scared.

They said the child turned towards the plane and saw the shell, dark, shining, like the muzzle of a monstrous animal; she felt something painful inside, something she didn't recognise, and she turned and looked at the man again, lifted her head, pushed her chest out and ran, forgetting the pain in her ankle, the water under the bridge and the air all around, suddenly burning and thin. 'Run, girl,' said the man in a low voice, 'keep going, you're nearly there, just a few steps' and he shut his eyes against the bomb, the glare and the power and the noise.

4

mary miller

Monday, 15 September . . .

And the dawn, Mary, you should see the great white dawn spreading over the desert, spreading and spreading; it's strangely peaceful here at dawn, gentle and peaceful. . . .

Monday, 28 October

The days are all the same. We march – fifteen miles yesterday – we run. There are conferences and reconnaissance missions, and we learn the maps by heart. Getting ready for war, dreaming that it'll never come. . . . Who'd want to be a part of it? Fox for one, the guy talks about nothing else.

12 November

Every day the temperature breaks new records; apart from that NOTHING. Got your parcel today. . . . Did I ever tell you I love you?

Still waiting, always waiting. For what? War, maybe. Waiting for war is a horrible thing. The guys are wound up all the time now. They say they can't wait for it to happen. I can. I've been learning 'petawnk' with some of the junior officers from the French battalion. At least I'll have learned something. What about you? Tell me what you've been up to. Go on, be nice to me, honey, I need something to kill the boredom. How's the dog getting along? And how's school? Is my saintly mom still bombarding you with plum cakes? Give Bonny my love.

25 December

Happy Christmas, hon. I miss you, if you knew how much I miss you, how much I love you. . . . Turkey for dinner tonight, can't see why they're not laying on a Yule log. I volunteered to be Jesus in the crib, but Roy was the only one who thought it was funny. Where are you spending Christmas? I think about you all the time. Love you. John.

1 January

Valentine Miller would like to wish you all the best for the New Year. Jewish on his father's side and Protestant on his mother's, Valentine hasn't been born yet, but I'm hoping to change all that as soon as I get home to you. Every night I think I hear the wind and rain rapping on the shutters of our bedroom window, but when I wake up you're not there. I'd like to go back in time and start all over again, but it wouldn't change anything, would it? Everything would happen just like before. So I give up and cup your breasts in my hands and touch them to my lips, my hands slide down over your stomach, my lips and my tongue follow, down between your thighs, where I tell you the *Thousand and One Nights*. Love me, Mary. John.

Thursday, 10 January

By the time you get this the war will probably have started. Every day the guys are more tense. At breakfast this morning Rodriguez said he wasn't going to die for a bunch of oil wells and the other guys called him a traitor – they ended up punching each other over it. Steward said we're here for the sake of democracy and justice. Half of them don't believe in that stuff any more. They're talking about Vietnam. . . . What am I doing here, Mary, what am I supposed to find out? I'm afraid of finding out what we're really doing here, scared of what I'll find out about me, about us. Tell me what's happening at home, tell me everything. I miss you all the time. I love you.

Wednesday, 23 January

This is it, honey. This time it's really happening. The planes went out and the bombs dropped. I don't know what to say. I just can't seem to find the words. What is there to say? That I'm okay, that I'm doing my job? I could tell you that the day after it all started they told us that we'd crushed the enemy and I believed them. That I was happy. Sorry, Mary, not happy exactly, it was victory, it was like a fire in my gut and I felt relieved it was all over. Just knowing that it was done, that we'd wiped them off the face of the earth, that we'd won and we could go home and the whole thing would be finished, and not thinking for an instant about the people under the bombs, not even for a second. . . . It woke me up in the middle of the night and it was then that I realised that this was just the beginning. The worst was still to come. The worst *is* still to come. And I felt scared. I panicked and I felt ashamed. I'm ashamed, honey. I'm sorry. Thanks for your letters. I think about you so much.

Monday, 4 February
. . . Everybody's tense all the time. You can feel it inside you day and night, in everything you say and in the way you move, the way that kids of twenty just lie down on the sand and fall asleep and never say a word. . . . They hadn't a clue what it would be like. And now they know, there's no way to turn it off. . . . I wonder what they'll be like afterwards?

Friday, 15 February
. . . They marched them past us, hands on their heads, their feet bleeding, some of them fell on their knees. You could see the terror in their eyes when they looked up at us. 'It's like using an H bomb to kill a fly,' said Bennet; he thought we were here to fight 'that sadistic motherfucking dictator' – that's what his commander told him – and finds himself up against men twenty years older than him who are worn out and just want to stay alive. I think Bennet's beginning to understand people. He's in shock, he doesn't know what to make of the word 'enemy' any more. He's scared of finding out that he's a killer. At least that makes one of us.

Sunday, 17 February, 11 p.m.
We moved to a new camp today. After dinner I went for a walk

as far as the dunes, there wasn't a light to be seen anywhere, just the desert whispering and rustling. Then it was quiet again. Like there'd never been a war, no kids screaming under the falling bombs, the dead weren't dead any more and we didn't have to think the worst. Then I remembered what we have to do tomorrow.... If you could see us, sometimes ...

Thursday, 21 February

I'm sick of seeing the guys getting out of their planes, shirts soaked in sweat and bragging about how many bombs they dropped. I'm tired of the rookies making up any shit just to pretend they're not scared. I think of you all the time, with the kids in the playground at school, I'm so jealous of you sometimes.

Monday, 25 February

The land offensive has been going on for twenty-four hours now.... Every minute I feel it snap like a trap behind me, there's no way out. It's like going through a hurricane and coming to the eye of the storm, where everything is calm and quiet, that's what the war feels like, like I'm in the war, like the war is me, am I making sense? I can see us all, Roy, Morrison, Franklin and the others. We're not the same, we'll never be the same now. Yesterday they were just guys, and now they scream and drive their tanks full tilt, their cannons rearing like a pitbull's prick, and get ready to shoot. We're running at each other, only a hundred yards between us and everything seems to stop for a second, like the second before the war started, not a sound, the silence is deafening, the earth stops spinning like nothing's happened yet and you feel like shouting 'it's okay, go home', but nobody would listen, they won't give up now, they'll fight to the death. It reminds me of a kid trying to join a gang. All summer he's wanted to hang out with these guys because they're cool and dangerous. He knows they'll treat him like a snot-nosed kid, tell him to go home to Mom, but he goes anyway. It's Saturday, his mom is at the hairdresser's and his dad is watching TV. He wants to join this gang so bad. As soon as he goes up to them they push him over, but he doesn't care, if he takes it, maybe in a week, or two, they'll let him be one of them. . . . We don't remember anything any more, Mary, we don't know shit any more. We're so far away. Don't forget me. I love you. John.

And then

3 January

Tonight, in the desert, I dreamed we were on a fairground ride. I felt your breasts against me, your legs, your hands, I was mad about you. I love you so much. Wait for me and I'll take you to Paris and we'll make love like we were never going to do anything else again. You're so beautiful when you undress. You're the most beautiful woman in the world when you come to bed, when you get up, when you make love . . .

Mary Rosanna Miller found out the war was over on 28 February on the eight o'clock news. It was a Thursday, outside it was raining. She put her mug in the sink and went out the back door of her wood-and-red-brick house, only yards from Bonny Fandall's almost identical one, in Provo,

Utah, USA. From her kitchen window Bonny saw her coming; she too had just heard the news and went outside.

The women met on the path and smiled, neither saying anything. The war was over. They didn't feel the rain on them. Then Bonny went inside and Mary Miller stayed there alone. She could think of nothing but the fact that John was coming home. She went back to her house, took off the jacket she was wearing – a man's jacket, John's in fact, which replaced her brothers' and her father's, which she had worn all her life. She put on a raincoat and went out again; there was no letter in the mailbox, and she thought about John again and decided to walk to school.

She went down Wilson Road past the lawns, freshly mown every Sunday, the sidewalk and the trees glistening with rain. Already some families had tied yellow victory ribbons around the bare trunks, to shutters, doors, windows, mailboxes, cars, baby buggies, everywhere; even wearing them on the backs of their jackets, but Mary Miller wasn't thinking about victory, she was thinking about John. The exile, like the war, was over. When John came home they would go away together; sometimes you have to get far away.

She didn't notice the mounting clamour in the streets of Provo, and the growing sense of excitement, a strange excitement on this strange day. On Abbey Road she met Mrs Wookpook and, a few yards on, the preacher's wife. She didn't have time to avoid them, their spreading, expansive smiles on their normally pursed faces, a triumphalism resounding in every 'dear' and 'darling'. Mary thought about the war as she watched these women – so certain they had won it – exulting 'ain't it a wonderful day?' then walked on to the school.

Flags were already fluttering, yellow ribbons hung from the windows and a posse of mothers rushed up to her, their little ones in their arms, saying, 'God be praised, isn't it wonderful news?' She imagined them only hours before hectoring their children, telling them to thank the Good Lord for such a miracle, for it was a wonderful day and Mary Miller wanted to feel John Miller's body in hers and wash away this vision of bleach-blonde mothers, hair sprayed firm for victory, without a flicker of peace in their smiles. The headmistress appeared in the porch and, as ever, Mary Miller couldn't help but think of the fat, flightless birds on the beach, harried by the children. The bell had gone for class, but the mothers showed no sign of leaving, so the headmistress cupped her hands to her mouth and shouted that the marvellous news didn't mean there wasn't work to do. 'We don't want our boys in the army to think we're slacking now, do we?' she added and some of the mothers felt a sudden surge of affection for this woman, who wanted her share of victory too. She clapped her hands and the playground emptied.

The cold drizzle clouded the classroom windows all day. Mary Miller thought of Wilson Road and the trees in Sandycove Square. As she came home, checking the mailbox to see if there was a letter from John, Howth barked and bounded towards her, still fastened to his chain. She threw on John's cardigan and sat on the sofa with a cup of black coffee to reread his letters, while she waited for Bonny to call round. She watched the news on CNN so she could hear it again, over and over, the war was over and John was coming home.

There was a photo of her and one of John next to the piano; on the coffee table a pile of books she hadn't opened since he went away, except *Ulysses*, which was always open at the same page, where sometimes she reread Molly Bloom's soliloquy: 'yes and first I gave him a bit of seedcake out of my mouth and it was leapyear like now yes 16 years ago my God after that long kiss I near lost my breath yes he said I was a flower of the mountain yes so we are flowers all a woman's body yes that was one true thing he said . . .'

Later that evening Bonny Fandall came round. They drank a bottle of French wine and ate pasta with garlic, and they didn't mention victory. Bonny sang an Irish song she had learned from her grandmother, about leaving and coming home. Before she went they talked about the picnics they'd have when the men came home. Mary Miller fell asleep holding one of John's letters, in which he told her about the desert and the red sand, of the endless nights and the war, like a knife-blade deep in the heart of day and night, and then she woke. Every night since he had left she woke. In the dark she thought about the dead children over there, of the women butchered and the old men crushed under the rubble of buildings that had stood for a hundred years, and she couldn't sleep.

235 Jackson Avenue, South Bronx, New York

Thanks for your letter. I was surprised when it arrived yesterday, after all these months . . . though I wasn't surprised by what you told me.

I'm not sure how to explain. I know you understand why I couldn't stay in the house, or in the town. The job I've got here is pretty much the same. I like the neighbourhood, it's about the only place in the world where I truly feel at home. I like the fact that it's so indifferent, I know the people here. I'll write properly in a little while. Look after your 'desert campaign'. Mary.

Sunday afternoon in the middle of a heatwave and the streets were deserted. Only a few old men and women with pushchairs sat on wooden benches between the red-brick buildings, waiting for the evening. The post office was a couple of blocks away. Mary Miller hesitated a moment before letting the letter drop into the box. As she dropped it she looked around – there were few buildings and fewer houses on Jackson Avenue as it meandered towards the East River; to the south some warehouses jostled for space with rusty water towers. Farther off was nothing but waste ground and rubbish tips, but no children, no shouts or yells; only a few groups of black teenagers and old women, sitting on the stoops of their houses, stared at her without interest. Mary Miller's hand remained poised, motionless, over the box; she could see the savage, slanted light of the sun over the desert dunes and the women veiled in black waiting silently behind her. A child laughed, she lifted her head, threw the letter into the post-box and headed home.

This had been her neighbourhood before: she'd lived on the corner of 149th Street and Jackson Avenue. It was an old T-shaped building, with a patch of waste ground fenced in with wire mesh. When she got back to her apartment she put a record on and closed the windows on to the childless square, and farther off the empty Bruckner Expressway. She stayed there a moment, looking off into the distance. She was wearing a black dress, cut low at the back, and heavy silver ear-rings; her hair was tied back, she held a cigarette. There was nothing but the music that filled the room: *Don Giovanni*, end of Act I. The walls were bare, not a painting nor a photo, nor a plant.

Mary Miller turned on the fan and got herself a cold gin-fizz. Donna Anna's voice cried: '*Per pietà, soccorretemi!*' Mary lay on the sofa and closed her eyes. The voice was heart-wrenching: '*Allora rinforzo i stridi miei, chiamo soccorso.*' Mary suddenly found herself thinking of the storm in Provo, a month after the war ended: the raging wind and the hailstones. The next day hundreds of birds lay dead on the banks of the lake. Leaves had been torn off the trees and slates from the houses, flowerbeds uprooted. She re-membered seeing soldiers, especially the younger ones, just back from the war, stand in the streets, motionless. Their shoulders hunched, their arms shielded their faces, insens-ible to people shouting their names, unsure if the streets of Provo and the desert they had left were not one and the same. Perhaps they felt the sand whipping them, heard the shells falling around them and then, at last, they looked up, looked around; and they remembered what they had done and walked on. All night the back door of the house banged against the frame. Thump. Thump. Thump. Cold air whistled through the rooms and in the morning the furniture was dusted with a fine layer of earth. A twin-engine crashed into the control tower, closing the airport for days. Even the trains stopped running. Mary Miller couldn't leave right away, she was forced to wait.

She picked up the letter again. It had arrived from France the day before.

... I went off to fight when I was twenty, with a knot of fear in my stomach, and in the end it became my whole life. Nobody would have guessed. Nobody. Just the opposite, in fact. War scared me as much as life itself. They put me on a boat. I'd never been away from home before. I spent the night on the bridge. I wasn't thinking about the war. I was thinking about my parents, about the farm I was leaving behind. That night I could feel the blood course faster in my veins, something opening up inside me, but the moment we got there I was sent off to an isolated mountain outpost and I felt scared again. Soldiers had been killed there only days before. I wasn't brave, I'd never been brave. I was sent out a week later. The second night we were fired on. I was lying in a clump of bushes, half dead with fright. I thought I was going to die. I couldn't move. One of the patrol, an Algerian, said: 'Is that all being alive means to you?' At the time I didn't understand what he meant, I thought it was an insult, but he laughed. 'You know the difference between a soldier who'll live and one who's going to die?' he asked. 'They're both shit-scared, but the one who's going to die trusts his fear, he trusts it more than he trusts life.' I looked at him, then I looked down. Something happened in me. If I were somewhere else, holding some girl's hand, I would have been sure what I was feeling was love. But here I was in some rocky outpost with a gun in my hand and what I was feeling was war. In the end I only felt at home at war, because that's where I first truly felt alive; if it had happened somewhere else I wouldn't be in the army. I stopped thinking about death. I discovered I was alive, I had a body and a name. It was there that I found myself. It was there that I first chatted up a woman. It was just a one-night stand, but I didn't care. Her name was Françoise. I still remember her. She took away another of my fears.

Going to war was like being alive, I couldn't tell the difference between the two; I couldn't live any other way. I got married, so there would always be someone waiting for me when I was sent away on a mission, but I lived for the missions. I came to love the fighting, body tense, throat dry, the sudden sense of being alive, like being in love, when nothing else matters; I even came to love the bullets, the rockets, the trembling bodies, the air ripping apart, the violence, the carnage, this was life. I loved the trap we were caught up in, I enjoyed the fear, the tiredness, the endless, sleepless nights and the dreamless sleep when it came. I didn't care about the why, I only cared about the heft of the weapons in my hands and against my shoulder, the bang as they went off, like a word that killed. When the order came to retreat I ran back. I liked the feeling of being far from everything, cut off from everything, of being alone, of everything at odds with what it means to be alive.

It never occurred to me for an instant that these moments were just troughs. I could have been killed, but others were killed instead; some of the bodies made me vomit where I was in the wasteland of gravel, but they didn't really touch me: not the limbs ripped off, nor the genitals stuffed in their mouths. Each death simply raised the stakes. War is a hateful thing for a man who does not love it. That's why some soldiers' faces are a blank slate. Perhaps haunted by the life before. But they go on, some of them, death piling on death, until they're no good for anything else any more. War is a grave to them. And the screaming children; it was the children who shamed me. I wanted nothing to do with savagery like that, but I didn't know anything else. I didn't want a normal life. I was sure I couldn't cope with it. This war was a defeat and that's one of the reasons that I carry on; it didn't matter whether we won or lost. . . .

Mary put the letter down. The music had finished. She thought again about the path winding through the desert and of the French captain who drove, sitting in silence beside her; she thought about the hotel and she closed her eyes.

Barely a week after the war had ended she stood, wiping the blackboard as the children filed out of her classroom. The headmistress came in, but Mary didn't understand at first why she was there in the doorway. Mary walked towards her but Cornelia Grossman stopped her with a wave and, without looking at her, said, 'Colonel Stark is waiting for you in my office.' She added, 'I'm so sorry.'

At that moment Mary Miller remembered that tomorrow she would be thirty-two. She even said it aloud, but the headmistress could find nothing to say.

Together, they walked across the playground in silence. The children's voices as they called out to each other reminded Mary of the videos taken from the planes during the bombing raids. You could see the sights and the path of the missile, then the building in the sights exploded. There was no sound, but in her mind she always heard shouting on the soundtrack.

The commander of the local military base, Benjamin T. Stark, greeted her by coming to attention, but did not offer his hand, and Mary, standing stiffly not a yard away, waited to hear the few words which would unravel the knot and which would never be said again. 'I'm so sorry,' he began, and he bowed slightly, but it was what came next that she wanted to hear, she wanted whatever pain and destruction was coming to be done. 'John Miller was reported missing in action,' he continued, but that was not the phrase she was waiting for.

She asked what it meant, 'missing'.

He answered, 'We have had no news of him.'

'For how long?'

'A week.'

'But the war was already over!'

'We believe it happened on the day operations concluded. He didn't return from his mission.'

'Was he on his own?'

'Yes. Alone.'

She asked where he was that day, what his mission was, what he was sent to do and why, how long it should have taken, what equipment he was carrying.

Benjamin Stark listened to her without interrupting, his cold eyes on her, he had already left. He had done what he came to do. He answered: 'Your questions relate to military operations which, I'm afraid, I am not permitted to discuss at present.'

She asked the questions a second time and the commander replied that they had instigated a search to find John Miller and would she please remain calm, there was no more to be said. He added that if John was not found after a reasonable time the army would consider her to be a war widow. 'Should it come to that, believe me, the army will do everything in its power to help you. I personally guarantee it,' he said to her, expecting no response. He handed her a list of agencies 'who can help you through this difficult time' and turned to thank Cornelia Grossman. The meeting was over.

Mary Miller pocketed the leaflet without reading it. It was standard issue, with details of the Vietnam war widows' association, a support group for partners of those missing in action and, somewhere near the bottom, an army psychological counselling service. Benjamin T. Stark took his leave, but not before hoping aloud 'that you have the terrible courage of trying not to wait', then he looked into her eyes, his face a mask of easy indifference and said, 'You're a very brave woman.' After he left, Cornelia Grossman told her she was sure that John would be found, that she must not give up hope, that he had probably been captured and that even if, God forbid, the worst had happened – she blessed herself and the sentence trailed off into silence. Vacation would start in less than a week, she said, she was sure Mary's class could manage without her. She would call, she said, to see if Mary had heard anything. She added, 'God looks after his own' and took Mary home.

In the months that followed the photos of John and Mary Miller remained on the piano in the living-room of the timber-and-red-brick house in Provo. Mary no longer played the Mozart sonatas, they left her fingers aching with a strange sense of disgust, of failure. On the coffee table lay the novels she used to read in the evenings; *Ulysses* still open at the same Molly Bloom monologue: 'yes he said I was a flower of the mountain yes so we are flowers all a woman's body yes that was one true thing he said . . .'

But on that day she lay on the sofa at home, wearing John's cardigan, the one which had replaced her father's and her brothers'. By the coffee table, Howth looked as though he were sleeping. She looked over at him from time to time. She knew what her future held; it was already here. She had taken the phone off the hook. For two or three hours she waited for the light to go on in Bonny Fandall's house. She knew that she must not move. If she moved, she would lose the game. It had happened before, a long time ago, but this time the stakes were too high, she had to staunch the pain and stop it from spreading inside her until it was too late. She closed her eyes. John was standing there, looking at her, and he started to cry. Howth whimpered then. After a while, John's face looking into hers, she fell asleep.

When she woke, three hours later, there was a light on in the Fandalls' house. She got up and went out the back door. The moment Bonny opened the door she knew, knew all too well, for she had known before Mary. Roy had called her from his base and told her that he'd waited all day for John to come back, but he never did. Bonny knew on that first night when the war ended and she sat silently with Mary through the long hours, hoping to ease the pain before it began.

She ushered Mary into the kitchen and took down a bottle of Black Bush. She made some sweet French toast and told Mary to repeat what Benjamin T. Stark had said, word for word. After the first words Mary stopped. Her face was a rictus of fear, her shoulders shook as though she were sobbing, but no tears came; she got up and Bonny thought she was leaving.

Outside, the lights in the houses flickered off one by one, soon there was only the glare of the street lights along the road and in the alleys. Bonny put her arms around her friend as though to rock her to sleep. She knew she could do nothing much to ease the terrible hurt, the nothing much was to give her all the comfort and the love she could, though she realised already that it would not be enough.

Late that night she walked Mary home. She turned on all the lights, leading Mary to her room, then she left. Mary wanted to be alone. She couldn't know that at that moment Ali ben Fakr, breathless, stumbled on the body of the young soldier. The war was over; he didn't want to hear another word about it.

Mary woke the next day as it was getting dark; for a second she forgot everything.

After the school holidays she started teaching again. The children had written a speech and done a drawing to welcome her back, and in the afternoon she took them to the zoo. The weather was perfect. The children threw peanuts to the polar bears and Marjorie Ford came up to her and asked if she was sad. Mary said that she was mostly worried about her dog, Howth, because he was alone all day and Marjorie walked away thinking about the dog, then she came back and told Mary that some day she'd like to have a dog too.

A few weeks later there was a parade to welcome back the 112th Company, John's company. The town turned out in force: there was a parade with majorettes and marching bands down Main Street, and streamers fluttered from the windows. Afterwards, there was a reception on the freshly mown lawns in front of the Town Hall. Everyone in the 112th Company was there in full military regalia, everyone but John. The night before they had been decorated by the US Government, but Mary wasn't invited. John was still just a missing person.

On the stand reserved for the families of soldiers Mary sat beside Bonny Fandall and watched the schoolchildren march past. Then the State Governor stood up to speak. 'America has triumphed,' he said, slapping his palms on the lectern in front of him, 'this is the beginning of a new world order, dedicated to justice and freedom throughout the whole world . . . and we pray for those brave and honourable men who died in such a noble cause; they gave their lives so that peace might reign; so that peace might spread to the farthest corners of the earth. Generations to come will remember them and cherish their memory; they will never be forgotten.' The 'Star Spangled Banner' rang out and the crowd, clearly moved, began to sing, then the Salt Lake City brass band sounded the 'Last Post', cold and sad, in memory of those who had fallen, but Mary wasn't listening. She was thinking about John.

It was Roy Fandall who had introduced them three years earlier. The very next day John had invited her to dinner in a small Tex-Mex restaurant outside town. They had barely sat down when he began to tell her about himself, about his father's garage in Brooklyn, his mother's work in social services. He talked about his relatives in Israel and about his time at college. 'It was Dad who wanted me to be an attorney, I didn't know what I wanted to do, so I gave it a try. At the time Roy was going on at me to join the army, but I said no way. You couldn't pay me enough to spend my life in the army. At the end of my first year I did some work experience in a big law firm in Manhattan and that's when I decided to give up. A couple of days later I went to see the recruiting officer at Roy's base. He talked to me about the sort of job I might do. I told him about my reservations and he just laughed. He was a nice guy. I joined up three months later, I still don't really know why I did it. That was two years ago.' Then he added, 'I suppose you're a pacifist.'

Mary didn't answer. She talked about her father, who was a Protestant pastor, about his parish in the Bronx, about how poor it was, how violent. She told him how, later, she'd joined a protest group – a radical movement – but she had left it a couple of years later. When she said this John was sure she wouldn't want to be with him.

The following day he called her and asked her out and she said yes. He took her to the Uinta National Forest and they had a drink at a small kiosk, and he told her all the Jewish stories he had learned from his father, who had learned them from his. He talked about his dad's garage, permanently full of old wrecks, and the rusty iron railings that ran around it.

He told her his father's favourite saying, which he told his son, in Yiddish, every year on his birthday: 'A humble man is just and victorious, riding on a donkey' and his mother's: 'I'd rather see my son with nothing but a donkey to his name, than see him kneel before strangers.'

When he walked her home that night, John held Mary Hart in his arms for a long time, then he pulled her to him, the length of their bodies pressed together and he made love to her slowly, silently. He was the first white man she had ever made love to. She was the first black woman he had been with.

A month before the war he sent a letter resigning his commission, but his call-up arrived the next morning, telling him he was to leave in less than a fortnight. Mary Miller received his last letter two days before the war ended: a few short lines about the death that was all around him, 'the brutal screams of men who seem to want to extinguish life and the memory of that life,' of 'hands that caressed on other days, weeks ago, maim and kill today', 'the war has made them faceless, blank . . . and those faces know peace is not worth the breath it takes to speak the word'.

As the high, sweet voices of the children of the Saint James choir sang out the 'Pater Noster', 'forgive us our trespasses and lead us not into temptation,' Mary Miller began to weep, her body cold and shivering as she watched some of the soldiers kneel on the cold ground, heads bowed, before praying that God might not lead them into the murderous temptation which they had given into so recently. She missed John so much she could barely stand   she missed his words   she needed to hear his voice   she wanted to heal his pain, to tell him that it was over   she wanted them to be together and to run from memorials and from victory parades, to forget the remorse of soldiers kneeling but victorious   she wanted him here, wanted to lay her hands on him and one by one remove the shards, close up the wounds opened by war, by death   everywhere the day broken by the screams of armed men   and the nights of sleep broken by fear and shame   she wanted to say she loved him, to say it again   to hear him laugh   to hear his fear subside   and her own.

The minister read a passage about the resurrection. He was careful in his short sermon to end on the word 'peace', reminding the congregation that they were dust in the first dawn and that unto dust they would return. The word called up the fine sands where they had been so recently, but they fought back the image. The service was over.

The lawn was laid out in its Sunday best, and the food sputtering on barbecues smelled of summer evenings and kerosene. Mary Miller looked around. Everyone seemed good-humoured, their homely victory celebration like a child's party, she searched the faces of the soldiers' families, grateful and contented as they stood by them. Children ran between the tables and the men talked gravely about world peace and about the coming harvest. She closed her eyes. Her body bowed, her knees buckled and the pain was there again, fresh and sharp.

A dead man flashed before her eyes, a dead man she had seen when she was eight years old. He had been stabbed in the back by a pimp who was no more than a kid, who simply walked away. Around him the women looked down, she heard one of them say 'nigger'. They turned away. They said nothing. Standing there, two streets from home, in the Bronx, for the first time she was unsure of who she was. This was why she had taken to the streets with her generation, fists raised, chanting 'Black is Beautiful', this was why she understood the generals and the colonels when they told their men to rape women in Vietnam. This was what made her like an exile at home, why she felt that she had no place. In the end, this was why she left for Provo where everyone who is not a Mormon is an outsider – black and white excluded equally. Then, one day, she met John. He was Jewish, she was black. He told her she was beautiful. He told her he could not bear to live apart from her and she believed him. For the first time she believed, and John Miller ended her exile so that she had a home wherever she might be. . . . But the war came back. And now, what they called peace, where men who had knelt moments before could laugh, because the people they had killed in the desert – niggers – didn't matter. Mattered hardly at all.

Now she was in exile again, she always would be. She couldn't fit in among the wealthy, well-fed men who talked about death with calculated indifference. She didn't fit in anywhere. She wanted to go and be with John wherever he was, dead or alive – what other home did she have?

Bonny called to her, she turned and Bonny said, 'Come on over, don't stand there all on your own' and she went to join them, pain nagging in her stomach and her legs trembling. All of John's friends were there, their uniforms freshly starched. They hugged her and told her how brave John was, what a good man he was, what a great guy; not one of them thought he might be coming home. She knew most of them; she could see they were happy to be there, to be safe.

Roy Fandall took her aside, and they went and sat at a table and for the first time she had news of John from someone who knew him, who had seen him. Roy told her that the last time he had caught sight of John was on the day the land offensive was launched, just before he went out, like the rest of them, on a routine mission. At first they didn't even worry when he didn't come back, but the war ended and he still hadn't returned to base. Roy asked around and discovered that the last time base had made contact with John was hours before the cease-fire. Then, nothing. There had been a sandstorm in the area he was headed for; maybe he had got lost. Unless something had happened to him. Nobody knew anything for sure.

Mary said that she wanted to go over there and asked if he would help her; he promised he would.

Tables were filling up around them and Mary wanted to leave. Roy said that he had something for her, but that he couldn't give it to her here. He asked if she would come to dinner the next day.

Mary sits, holding the empty gin-fizz glass. She gets up and throws the windows wide. The sweltering New York heatwave blasts into the room, and instantly she remembers the hot humid nights on the gravel plains near the border, of night on the deserted beaches in K., black from the burning oil wells and the sleepless nights in the hotel, cold and heavy like long winter nights, her body twisted with tiredness and broken by the immense loneliness, so vast, so hopeless, that it seeps from her as shame, as thirst. She thinks about John, about the cairn on the dune and the harsh, dusty wind whipping over the stones. She goes out.

She takes the subway to Brooklyn, knowing they are always home on Sunday afternoon. Coming out of the subway, she buys flowers and a cake.

It is her mother-in-law who answers the door. She opens her arms. 'Come in,' she says, 'come in, darling.' She always says the same thing. She thanks Mary for the flowers and the cake and adds, 'You really shouldn't have.'

They look at each other, barely a glance, but enough to see the tiredness and loneliness in each other's faces. Lea says, 'It was good of you to come.' She calls out the window to Samuel. Mary leans out and watches him working under the hood of the long white Bentley riddled with rust and age. He waves to her and, as always, she wonders if she should have come. He changes, comes into the room and says, 'Hello, hello.' He kisses her, then stands looking at her and says, 'I prayed for you on Friday.'

She doesn't know what to say; since she came back to the Bronx they have all tried not to say anything that will dig up the past. All the same, she asks: 'You prayed for me?'

'Yes.'

'Did you ask God to fix my TV set?'

He smiles and lights his pipe.

Lea Miller carries in plates for the cake. 'What were you saying?'

'Samuel says he prayed for me on Friday, but he won't tell me what he prayed about.'

Lea looks down. 'That serious, huh?'

'It's nothing serious, honey,' Samuel Miller says. 'Nothing serious. I just prayed for a bit of help.'

'For me?'

'No, for me.'

'But I thought you were praying for me?'

'I was.'

'I thought by now you'd have noticed that it doesn't work.'

'Maybe, maybe not.' He looks up at her, his eyes smiling. 'Let's pretend it does, eh?'

The simple phrase suddenly makes Mary want to cry. She stands: 'If we're going to wait around for miracles to happen, maybe we should have some cake in the meantime?'

'I wasn't praying for a miracle. Didn't your dad ever tell you you're not supposed to pray for miracles?'

'I probably forgot.'

'I didn't pray to forget, either. I'm sure your dad told you there's no such thing – it's like daisies in the desert.'

She wipes this last word from her memory and says again: 'You really won't tell me what you prayed for?'

'What if it didn't come true?'

Lea Miller puts a steaming teapot on the table and tells them to sit. She hands Mary a slice of cake and sits down. They sit in silence. Mary notices that they have taken down the photo of John from the sideboard, but says nothing.

Lea and Samuel look at each other, Lea clears her throat and sips her tea. She is the one who tells Mary that they are moving away. They have found someone to buy the garage. She could still come to see them whenever she wanted. Samuel's nephew could get her the plane tickets cheap. Then she says that they weren't sure at first, that they wanted to stay, for her sake, but they were too old. They had to go. She stops, then adds: 'Don't be mad at us.'

Mary says nothing. In her head, she counts out the dead and the departed and says: 'It's okay, I'll marry a fireman from Oklahoma and take up cycling professionally.'

Samuel looks at her, his face sad and says: 'We wanted to leave the car with you, if that's okay?'

She nods. Lea tells her they would be leaving in two months.

Mary says simply: 'I think you're doing the right thing' and takes another slice of cake.

They go for a walk together in the evening through East River Park. Lea lends Mary a white linen jacket and against the ground she looks like a melting snowflake.

'You're a beautiful girl,' says Samuel. When she didn't reply, he adds: 'When my son came to me and announced that he'd met you he was stammering so badly I didn't even think to ask if you were Jewish. And I would never have thought to ask about the colour of your skin. He just said, "I've met Mary Hart," as though you were someone I'd known all my life. And I said, "Oh, her, yes . . . I've read all about her in the papers" and he just said, "yes, that's the one." He wasn't joking, you know, I was stunned, I knew then that it had to be serious. You spend too much time on your own, Mary.'

'Leave the girl alone,' says Lea, 'what would you do?'

He's about to say, 'I would sign up', but bites his lip. 'I'd become an umbrella salesman.'

Lea shrugs.

'And you?' he said.

'I'd probably have waited.'

'To grow old?'

'No. I don't know, it's a stupid question, leave the girl in peace.'

Samuel puts his arm around Mary's shoulders and tells her that he loves her. All around them, the sky blazes white with the promise of snow, but it's only the smog.

When she got home, Mary poured another gin-fizz and put on the same CD. She thought about what Lea had said, about waiting, then she picked up the French captain's letter again and began reading: 'There are a lot of ways of losing a war. You can be killed, or come back crippled, or one day you can stop loving it. Maybe then you finally see it for what it really is. . . . John saw war for what it really was, it hurt him just to be a part of it. At the time I didn't understand. To me, it was a war like any other. It was only afterwards that I saw it differently, maybe I just saw all wars differently. . . .'

It was raining outside. Mary picked up the telephone and dialled, and heard the ringing tone echo in space. Donna Anna cried, *'Don Ottavio, son morta!'* Mary lay down on the sofa, her hand resting on her stomach, and waited for day to break.

At about six, she put on the white linen jacket and went out. The old man in the Greek corner shop had already opened up. When he saw Mary go past, he came to the door and called her; he asked if she would have coffee with him.

As they sipped the coffee, the old man told her how he had first seen Liberty Island from the deck of an old cargo ship, the *Felicitad*, sketched in the fog of New York harbour. '1928, it was,' he said. 'You weren't even a glint in your poppa's eye.'

Mary Miller thought about the neatly clipped lawns all along Wilson Road, the trees in Sandycove Square. She thought about Cornelia Grossman, standing in the doorway, hand on the door handle, saying, 'I'm so sorry.' She looked at the old man and smiled, then she left the shop.

5

the defeated (iii)

It was not a dream about women, of a woman lying across him, her legs spread, like the dreams Abou Salem sometimes told him in the mornings, it wasn't one of the old nightmares that had haunted him, where he fell endlessly into a void; this was a dream of the war.

In it, he is lying in the shadow of a tank, the sun spills down directly overhead, he is dozing. A sharp noise makes him turn, he stands, his comrades are gone, there is nothing but a train of ammunition on the sand.

He takes a few steps, walks around the tank towards the sound. Then he sees them, standing, smiling, motionless only a few feet away. She wears the veil she always wears for travelling, the silver threads glittering in the sunlight, he is wearing an old keffiyeh. He is carrying a basket and a bag.

He hesitates. He cannot believe they are here, they would have had to cross half the country, but the man opens his arms and he walks towards him, never once looking away from his eyes, and feels his arms close around the man's shoulders, feels the rough, familiar stubble and smells the familiar smell. He seems thinner, somehow, but he says nothing; asks no questions.

At last, he hears his voice. Soft, at first, barely a murmur or a prayer, he can barely hear what he is saying, then his voice is clearer, more defined, and the flood of words spilling from his mouth talk of God and of these lost months, of fate, of the war that came down like the fall of night. He talks of luck and how close it is to misfortune, and the strength a man needs just to remain standing. He talks, too, about the days before he left, of the house echoing with his absence, of the worry that sometimes keeps him awake all night and of his coming home soon; he talks about musicians he will invite to the homecoming, calling them by name, describes the fatted calves that will be meat to their table, reckons the prayers that he will offer up to celebrate his return. There will be the most magnificent party he has ever thrown.

While he talks, she watches him in silence; now he breaks free of the embrace and goes to her. Her hair has grown grey, but he tells her she is more beautiful than he remembered just to see her smile and say, 'Come, now, you know that's not true.' He lays his face against her neck so that she can stroke it. He can feel her skin, wrinkled like an overripe fig.

She seems gentler than he remembered and he tells her so without lifting his head. He can feel her chest contract and he knows she is crying. He says, 'Thank God you're here' and hugs her. She says his name, over and over, as though she cannot find anything else to say, so he kisses her and kisses her again.

They sit, then, in the shadow of the tank and he tells them about the war. He says nothing of the loneliness, of the endless waiting, of the urgent need he feels to run away, of his feet, bloating in the heat, of the fear that wakes him with a jerk in the early hours; he tells them about battles that never were, about liberating towns that appear on no map, he talks of how he captured prisoners of war and how grateful they were for his mercy. He gives these men names, sketches their faces, enumerates the weapons they carried when he captured them, every detail, down to the children they never had in the name of whom he spared their lives. After a while his mother interrupts and asks if he is hungry. In answer he turns to his father and says that the supplies don't always arrive on time and watches his father nod, remembering his own hunger in another war.

She picks up the basket they have brought. In it is some flat bread she has kneaded and fried, onions she has cooked for hours reducing them to a dense marmalade, some dates and figs, and some rice with mutton. He is hungry. They hardly feel the heat beating down on them. He puts a piece of meat in his mouth and remembers his house shrouded in vines, his school and the street where he played with his brothers when they were alive, he remembers the interminable stories his father's father would tell in the evenings, the water glinting in the well, the dark eyes of Soraya, the woman he was to have married.

When he woke, Abou Salem was snoring beside him. All around him night stretched out like a bottomless dark well. He was hungry and cold. He could hear nothing, so he went out and walked around the tank to the place where they sat, to see if they had left traces in the sand.

6

the french captain

The window opens wide on to a country road in the half-light and farther off stretch bare fields stripped by the harvest. A nightingale sings somewhere in the dark, the sound of regret lodged in its throat; Robert Nantua listens, motionless. He lies, stretched out, his penis limp. He can feel desire course elsewhere; in his hands and fluttering in his skin, and he remembers the skin of the woman next to his. One night had been enough to wipe out thirty years, thirty useless years. Her body beneath him, her eyes watching him, but she is trying to hold on to her life, to remember. Every day he recollects this. This is the reason he left, why he gave up the war and the day-to-day monotony of his life. He had never spoken to anyone about it, never said a word until she came. Everything about her told him life was something different, though she never said a word, but he understood just the same. He had only to look at her to understand. He had lost everything to her and he ran away. He ran away to hide. He didn't want the things he had before: the hands that carried guns, the voice for shouting orders, toy soldiers. He missed her, now that she was gone. Like him, she belonged to no one. There was a time when she had belonged, there had never been such a time for him. She did not love him, but some women will love in spite of anything. She said life is something different; nobody had ever said this to him before. He believed her and felt his fear subside, but not his pain.

'I don't know what victory means any more,' he said, as they said their goodbyes in the barrack square. It was a year after the war ended, the men then under his command could not even look him in the eye now. His military career was over.

Three months later he started divorce proceedings. His friends were surprised, convinced there must be another woman. He let them talk. He left most of his money and his belongings to his wife and sons. Everything but the farm in Saône-et-Loire where he was born during the war. He moved in the very week that Mary Miller left Provo for the Bronx, but he didn't know that. He traced her some months later through the register at the military base in Provo; he was unsurprised to find that she had left.

Six months later he wrote to her. He sent many letters, but she only received the first. He did not give her his new address and she did not reply. Still, he continued to write.

The day the war ended he was with his men in the desert. He had received the news just before dawn, a few words: 'Immediate Cease-fire – Halt Advance', probably. The men were still sleeping. He walked out. Outside there was barely a glimmer of day. He looked across the dark desert, thinking nothing; then, without quite knowing why, he said to himself that this war would be his last and he went to tell the men. He waited until they were standing to attention for inspection, then he said simply, 'The war's over.' There was silence for a moment, then a howling cacophony. Some of them screamed, others buried their faces in their hands, for the first time he thought about the defeated.

A few hours later they headed back across the desert. The young soldiers were standing on their tanks, dancing and laughing and swearing they would never set foot in this fucking desert again. They shook their heads wildly, like children; they had got out alive – there was no feeling like it.

Ten days later they were back in France. As the Transall touched down on the runway the men fell silent. Robert waited until the plane had stopped, then went into the aisle and called each of them by name. Once on the ground, some ran off; others stood, dazed, as though they didn't know where they were going any more. Watching them, Robert remembered the first time he had come back, more than thirty years ago.

After they had disembarked he stayed alone on the plane, unable to think, as he was every time; his lips were dry, his heart hammered   every time he came back   this time,

more urgently   a sudden sense of uselessness   his life
        everything he was   a lie: for an infinite moment,
everything was incinerated   his wars like dead letters
        he couldn't live as others did   he had no trade, no
education   like an amputee   what then?   back to
war   again   what else?   his throat tightened   his
eyes cold and wet   a stranger defeated   condemned   to
live.

Rain thrummed on the cabin roof; outside someone called
to him. He heard a voice. It called again. He said 'Coming'
and for the first time in his life he counted out the years since
he had first gone to war.

He thought back to the interminable afternoon briefings
spent preparing for war, in the sweltering heat of the tents; to
the laminated maps strewn on the ground, he pointed out
the names of villages and dunes where they had no reconnaissance information, moving the red and black stickpins
across invisible roads, tracing arrows that conjured the
troops moving, circling their targets, all the while repeating
the well-worn clichés that served in every conflict; he
thought about the days spent shifting mountains of sand
and digging cliffs into the dunes to make it easier to move the
tanks through, though no one knew where or when the
battles would be fought. He remembered the night the land
offensive was launched. He had been out in the desert, he'd
scribbled the exact time in his notebook. At that moment
there was still peace – he had forgotten the wars which had
come before. Now the order had been given to fight and he
in turn passed it on. The tanks moved out, crushing a path
across the land; he watched the plumes of sand, the men

running and shouting, going to fight, to die, to kill. He could remember every detail about that night, the precise colour of the sky, dark, almost violet, and of the men gathered before him about to set off, silent, shoulders stiff. He had always followed orders to the letter and ensured that others did the same; the hundreds of men under his command like lead soldiers to be positioned on maps, on battlefields. He had given lectures on the subject: 'Never forget that the lives of those under your command depend on your courage and on your ability to remain clear-headed.' He had been scrupulous in his respect for authority and that in itself was his reward. Never once in those thirty years had he stopped to ask himself what sort of life this was.

His wife and sons were waiting for him in the VIP lounge at the military airport. He saw them wave to him from far off; his sons standing stiffly, hesitant of running to meet him. He didn't know whether to hug them to him or shake their hands.

His wife came and pressed her face against him, it was a gentle face, the face of someone rarely noticed. He felt a sudden tenderness towards her, but no spark of desire.

That night, and the nights that followed, he told them stories. He spoke about the soldiers he'd defeated and the battles he had fought. The crushing victories among the dunes, the strategies of war. He described the desert reddening under the dawn and the sandstorms, the stray dogs in the deserted villages and the clouds of sand that halted the tanks. He tried his hardest to conjure images for his sons that would bring back their childish faces. He told them about the young pilots coming back from their missions, their hands still shaking with fear, and how the fear faded when they were welcomed as heroes and they looked suddenly as though they had just remembered that they had always been on the winning team. He told them about their rapid advance through the desert, about taking an outpost, about the mines and the wounded. His sons sat, saying nothing. Sometimes he embroidered the tales to see them lean closer to him and the story raced along; he knew that afterwards there would be no more.

Some days later he went to Paris for a meeting at the Ministry of Defence. He left the Ministry at 4 p.m. and walked through the streets, his mind and face a blank. Two weeks previously he was charging across the desert, attacking the bald dunes, the deserted outposts, while here, everywhere, on the bridges and the river banks, on the Place du Carousel and on the lawn of the Tuileries he saw couples kissing, children running around the statues chased by women in light dresses. The city was wrapped in an unseasonal spring, it almost glowed: the cathedrals and the statues, the squares and the angels, arms raised in supplication in the city light. It was as though the dunes had never existed, there had been no tanks, no desert; no city in the world could shrug off history so quickly. Under the chestnuts blossoming there was already the heady scent of post-war evenings. Young girls sitting on the café terraces gossiped about new boyfriends, the crowds gathered as usual on the boulevards and the old women sitting on the park benches closed their eyes and remembered the first time they had felt this sudden gentle relief, and the city stood suddenly, a little drunk, watching the heady march of the victors.

He watched the evening news in his hotel room; looked at the soldiers coming back from war, down the gangways of the aircraft carriers, along the asphalt of the military runways, their backpacks on their backs, waving to the cameras or making a victory V, while others passed, silent, anonymous. Robert Nantua remembered the howls of victory in the desert and remembered his own home-comings, especially the first. He had never found the words to describe the long days watching for men in the undergrowth and trying to kill them. Every time he tried, silence interrupted.

He wondered what the people he had passed in the streets thought about this homecoming. Did they wish the war forgotten now that it was over? Did they think of their own youth? Of the defeated? Did they think about peace? Of the relief of simply being able to say, 'It's okay, everything is okay'? Maybe, and maybe that is what brought them out into the streets in their thousands, in the big cities and the small provincial towns, their children riding on their shoulders to see the soldiers come home.

When the ordinary soldiers saw the crowds waiting for them outside the ports they were stunned. They wondered if all these people had turned out for them. Women gave them flowers, hands stretched out to shake theirs, flags waved and imperceptibly the soldiers threw back their shoulders and walked on; perhaps this was what victory meant. In the barracks squares they met their families. As they held one another, the soldiers felt the ground slip out from under them. The film crews were waiting for them in the hangars, the journalists going through the motions as they had done all through the war: they asked for the soldiers' opinions, their impressions, but the soldiers had nothing to say. In each man's mind an image of the desert rose, unbidden, and each felt a sharp pain in his chest. He didn't know what he was doing any more, but turned to his mate, climbing over the tanks hauling dust sheets and tool boxes and other gear. He shouted out to him: 'Pierre!' The name rang out in the hangar. His mate looked up, smiled. 'How's it going, mate?' He nodded. 'Everything okay? You sure?' His mate laughed. 'I'm fine, give me a fucking break!' Their voices melded in the echo from the corrugated iron roof. Down the chain of men they passed their gear, of no importance now, and they bragged about girls; quick to behave as though they had never been away. They waited to forget about the war; each man knew that one day he would no longer be able to forget.

Back in Paris, Robert Nantua's first duty was to write a report on the movements of his division during the offensive. Facts and dates: troop numbers; precise co-ordinates in the desert; troop morale, the state of the equipment, his thoughts on the lines of communication. How well had the allied command structure worked during the offensive? What about discipline? Appraisals of the non-commissioned officers. Assessment of objectives. A week later he had still not started.

The log he had kept during the war lay open on his desk. Sometimes he would jot down a phrase or two, but he crossed them out immediately. From his window on to the courtyard he watched the low, gun-metal sky over Châteauroux and the bare barrack trees, and was perversely reminded of the harsh desert light, the heat, the colours of the dunes at evening; the overcast skies. They were not memories of the war, but of day breaking on the dunes, of the clear, luminous air and the mornings; each time he thought about it he felt the same sharp pain in his chest. He missed it, all of it. One morning he decided to finish his report once and for all. He sat at his desk for a full ten hours, never once getting up. By evening it was finished.

The barracks was deserted now of all but a handful of active platoons. He reread the report in his barracks room and his huge laugh rang around the deserted buildings. He had mapped out with military exactitude the twenty-two weeks of waiting and fighting; not a number nor a detail was missing, each day of the war ground through the mill of his formidable military analysis; but the ground trembling under the bombs, the sleepless nights, the men screaming in the dunes and the dead, the hatred and the sudden bursts of laughter were left out. There was no trace of them in the closely typed pages, nothing, and for the first time it occurred to him that war was all about missing words.

It was 1 a.m. Robert asked to be put through to the head of his mine-sweeping team, who was still at the base. It took half an hour, the operator put the call through and called him back. It was obvious that he had dragged Adrien Froissard out of bed. He apologised, explaining that there was no special reason for calling, he just wanted to ask how things were, if he was all right. The line was bad and he didn't hear Adrien's reply, so he apologised again and hung up, then went to the window and saw that it would be hours yet before dawn.

The next day he handed in his report and made a presentation of his conclusions. Easter would be upon him soon and he would go and spend a few days with his family in Saône-et-Loire. He would go walking over the hillsides festooned with vines, go to his window at night and see the half-lit road and the fields stretching out beyond, feeding on the heavy silence of the fat land. And forget.

The night before he left there was a knock at his door and a warrant officer he didn't know gave him an urgent message. Robert read it, checked to be sure that it was addressed to him, then reread it. It was from de Matre at Military Head-quarters: 'Contact the Ministry urgently, extension 6144. You leave on mission in forty-eight hours.' There was no explanation. Robert called Frederic Renand, but the lieutenant-colonel knew nothing more than that orders had come directly from Paris. A little later he called the Ministry and was told that de Martre would be out all day. An NCO at extension 6144 confirmed the message. A seat had been reserved for him on a plane leaving the following day. The officer gave him the flight details, adding only that the mission might last some weeks.

His wife, Thérèse, cried when she heard that he was leaving again, and cried again when he drove her and his sons to the station the next day. He couldn't find the words to say . . . His ticket arrived later that morning, as arranged. Only the departure date was marked and the destination: the city of K. The desert.

He unpacked his things from the trunk where his wife had so carefully packed them. His khaki shirts and his shorts smelled of mothballs. He stuffed them into a bag and left, forgetting his toiletries and the letter he had written to his wife. He didn't remember them until it was too late. Outside it was raining. He hailed a cab. The driver was an old black man, silent as death. Robert laid his head back against the seat and closed his eyes. The windscreen wipers beat a jagged rhythm over the music blasting from the radio. The driver offered to turn if off, but he shook his head and pushed himself deeper into the seat.

Images of the war had flickered through his mind all night: waiting, screaming on the dunes, grabbing his men by the scruff of the neck and screaming that this wasn't a fucking playground and forcing them to crawl ten minutes more because he had seen a glimmer of fear in them, moving troops in total darkness; each night feeling the space close a little tighter around them, speaking in low voices until finally they were silent, the sky, impossibly vast, opening above them each morning, and his homecoming in France, his fear of being home. It was a jumble of sensation: leaving–fighting–coming home – always finding the will to live somewhere else.

He had dreamed of himself, sitting in the desert on a stone chair, and the image woke him. He had stared at his wife beside him and wished she would turn to him, nestle between his legs and refuse to let him go, but she slept on.

He arrived at the airport early and called his wife, but he was clumsy and awkward, he tried to ring back and thought he would write to her. Then he forgot.

The plane was half empty. He sat at the back of the cabin by the window. A fat man smelling strongly of cigar smoke sat next to him. Robert thought about changing seats, but the plane was about to take off. He took out a copy of *The Man*

Without Qualities, a book he had bought years ago for its title and which he'd never read – probably because of its title.

All around him men in summer suits kept up a steady commentary about the contracts they hoped to secure out there, now that the war was over, the rebuilding work had opened up important new opportunities in construction. He started to read: 'The lady and her companion had also come close enough to see something of the victim over the heads and bowed backs. Then they stepped back and stood there hesitating. The lady had a queasy feeling in the pit of her stomach, which she credited to compassion, although she mainly felt irresolute and helpless. After a while the gentleman said: "The brakes on these heavy trucks take too long to come to a full stop." This datum gave the lady some relief, and she thanked him with an appreciative glance.'

When Robert's neighbour asked him for a light he barely reacted. The man leaned over, inspecting his book, and asked him why he was travelling. He questioned Robert about his rank. 'A captain, eh? I would have put money on it,' he said. 'So, Captain, going back to the scene of the crime? Oh, don't mind me, I say that, but I wasn't against the war . . . bloody awful mess all the same . . . still, these things happen from time to time . . .'

'I'm going there to be decorated,' Robert interrupted and turned to the window. Fleetingly, he saw the faces of his sons and wondered what kind of a father he was; then he fell asleep.

The plane had just reached the edge of the desert when he woke. Below, he saw the endless grey sand stretched out, ground he had covered during the war: sand raked by a handful of dry riverbeds, clumps of coarse grass, the stony plains and the vast sky. There was no trace now that any human being had ever been there and he suddenly felt claustrophobic in the plane. He wanted to go back, to be down there, under the dense heat. He closed the book. The sky was turning red and Robert Nantua looked out at the boundless blood-red sky; it reminded him of war.

The plane began its descent. Robert leaned back and thought, oddly, of the American communications officer who had come to their camp one night. It had been just before the land offensive. They had had dinner together, just the two of them, in his tent. Robert had offered him a good vintage burgundy which he seemed to appreciate, and they talked about the war. The younger man told him how every night, in the mess hall, a young assistant engineer, Tony Accompt, chalked up the number of bombs dropped that day, and how they took turns drawing the silos they had bombed and the bridges they had wiped out. He mimicked them sketching; Tony, a small, fat kid with red hair, standing on a stool, trying to line up his figures, then someone else, a stocky black guy, mapping out the targets they had hit above the numbers. He had mimicked the pilots standing up in turn, yelling out their scores for the day and then he'd sat down and said that he didn't find it funny at all. Robert had said nothing.

After they had eaten they walked around the deserted camp. The American had talked about New York and Utah, where he lived now, about his wife and how he missed her and then, in his awkward French, he had apologised for talking too much. Robert had told him about his time in the army, his years at war, adding, inexplicably, that some men were better off out of it. The American had asked then if he liked his job, and he'd nodded.

'And you like war?'

'Yeah, and war.'

'Why?'

'Stops me getting bored, I suppose.'

'And that's enough?'

'Yeah – it's enough for me, anyway.'

'It's strange, I find war horribly boring.'

He had fallen silent, then apologised for asking the question.

Robert had smiled and said he didn't mind. 'You know, you can dedicate your whole life to war and still envy people who stayed out of it.'

The young officer had looked at him. 'Do you regret it?'

'No. I don't think so.'

A little later he had said that when he got back to America he would resign his commission and he and his wife would go and live in another state.

'What will you do?'

'I don't know yet.'

The moon, a deathly white, shone over them.

'You're right to get out of the army,' Robert had said, before offering him a nightcap.

The young officer had left just before dawn; he'd turned to thank Robert. 'There's something wrong, chief.' he'd said, 'something wrong.' Robert had not seen him again.

His plane touched down.

Stepping on to the walkway, he stopped, felt the air

outside, bloated and hot, and was glad that he was here. Someone from the embassy was waiting for him on the runway. Robert noticed the first silhouettes of women, veiled completely in black, and the sky overcast from the burning oil. They quickly crossed the city – a startling mix of futurist skyscrapers, opulent palaces and ugly houses – moving in a jerky rhythm along roads peppered with craters, endless detours and bombed-out bridges; the rebuilding was only beginning.

The ambassador welcomed Robert personally, congratulating him on the work of his mineclearing squad. Their mission had been extended but that, the ambassador said, was not why he had been asked to come. The high command had elected Robert to take charge of the files of those missing in action. 'I realise', the ambassador said, 'that none of our own boys are missing, but it's important to help our allies in this. You were the obvious candidate – your knowledge of the terrain is second to none. The list of the missing runs to eighty men; you'll be given a quarter of the files. Needless to say, you have *carte blanche* to organise things as you see fit. The allied embassies are putting their resources at your disposal. You'll have a permanent pass and a team of two men. If you need back-up, we can provide men from those stationed here. One more thing,' he added, 'I'd like you to meet someone. She flew in last night from the US. She's just next door.'

Robert watched as a slim black woman entered the room. 'I'd like to introduce Mary Miller. Her husband is among the missing.'

part two

7

somewhere in a desert (ii)

Mary Miller and Robert Nantua parted company on the steps of the town hall in Rijna, as arranged. Robert wanted to question the authorities about any bodies that had been found in the area, while Mary went through the town with a sheaf of pictures of John.

When she had shown the photo to Robert that first evening he recognised the man immediately: it was the American officer he had been thinking about on his flight here. Miller, that was his name. In the photograph he was smiling.

He taught Mary what to say when she showed people the photograph, some approximation of 'Do you recognise this man?', which she learned by heart. It had been a week since then and she had said it a hundred times. They had stopped in fifteen villages since leaving K. Each time, he questioned the civil and military authorities, while she spoke to dozens of people in the street, but they learned nothing. There was no word of any men missing in action and none of John.

The village they had stopped in the night before was on the other side of the border, but Mary persuaded Robert to go on. In the end he agreed. When John Miller disappeared there was a sandstorm blowing; he could easily have crossed the border without noticing. 'One more day,' Mary said. 'There's a village just on the other side of the border; it can't be more than twenty miles. If we don't find anything there we'll go back.'

Driving across the border the next morning, they passed a deserted border post and Robert stopped in the shade to check the map, then they drove on. Neither noticed the spectacle case, half buried in the sand beside the open doorway.

They quickly left the flat plains of sand, which circled the border like a belt, and headed west towards the dunes. Though it was riddled with craters, the road had been recently resurfaced – proof that foreign troops had passed this way, but any other sign of their passing had been rubbed out by the sand. The banks that sheltered their camps had disappeared and the charred firewood along the roadside could have been left there by nomads, who were already reclaiming their seasonal routes.

As they passed, Robert recognised, very precisely, a spot where he and his men had made camp for the night. They had put up their tents nearby, away from the roadside. The men had played cards; steeling themselves for crossing the border; for the battle ahead; there was nothing now to tell of their passing in the monotony of sand and dry riverbeds, and the deserted roads.

When they came to the first dunes, a light breeze blew veils of sand. As they rounded a difficult bend the jeep began to lose traction; they were in the dunes themselves now: hundreds of hills flesh coloured and gold stretching before them as far as they could see, covering the horizon, blocking out the sky. Robert stopped the jeep and Mary got down, took a few steps and stopped. All around, dunes rose up, like the heavy flanks of an animal turned towards the sky; they were everywhere and they were beautiful. The air lifted wisps of white dust from their tips. Everything here was hostile to man, it pushed him back or tripped his feet, and for the first time Mary could imagine John, alone here in this place. She didn't hear Robert call her at first; it was only a couple of miles now to Rijna and he wanted to be there by noon.

They said nothing until they got to the village. Robert parked the jeep outside the office of the local authorities and watched as Mary Miller went on her way, certain that she would find out nothing.

Mary walked down an alley where she had seen a little girl, carrying bread, waiting in a doorway. She turned when she heard Mary coming. Mary took the photo from her bag and walked towards the child; she held it out and repeated what Robert had taught her. The girl looked at the photograph silently, carefully, and shook her head: 'La, la.' No. She didn't recognise him. She looked at Mary again and turned away.

In the next street Mary stopped an old woman as she left her house, then two young girls further down the street; they didn't recognise him. She took a third street and a fourth; through the half-open doors she could glimpse courtyards, and the shadows of women and children coming and going, but she did not dare to go in. Stairs arched across the old town; everything was closed and silent. The heavy wooden doors glowed hard blue, almond green and warm ochre. The sand beneath her feet muffled her footsteps; only an old man passing with a donkey, or children shouting, broke the silence, which immediately closed around her again.

It was warmer now, soon the houses would close up, one by one, until late in the afternoon and she had still not found anything. Robert was probably right, they had gone too far, foreign armies had barely passed this way, there was no reason for John to have come so far. She sat on a stone at a crossroads. The few men who passed stared at her, but she didn't notice them. She had only an hour before she was due to meet Robert. She stood up. She had noticed a palm grove a little further on, which ran around the old town; at least there she might find a little shade.

The palm grove was lined with high-walled houses. Mary saw a woman, veiled in black, about to enter. She walked faster. When the woman saw her she stepped back, but Mary walked up to her, held out the photograph and repeated, 'Have you seen this man?'

The woman ran her gnarled old thumb over John Miller's face. She seemed to have forgotten that Mary was waiting, then she looked up into Mary Miller's eyes and nodded, and very softly, she said 'nam (yes)'. Mary was unsure she had heard the woman and she repeated: 'Have you seen this man.' The old woman looked down and motioned Mary to follow her.

The door opened on to a dark corridor. The old woman leaned against the wall as she walked. They came to a courtyard where three women were sitting on stone benches around a fountain. They stood up and the woman spoke quickly to them, pointing to Mary. The youngest came over and, in halting English, welcomed her.

One of the women went inside, and Mary turned to the girl and held out the photograph. The girl stepped back a little when she saw it. As she did so, the woman came out again, carrying a tray with tea and fruits. When she saw the photograph she dropped the glass she was holding and it toppled on to the flagstones. The other women turned. Light glittered on the spilled tea. Mariam, the youngest, stood motionless; Mary Miller waited. Heavy, irregular breaths of suffocating heat came from outside; Mary went and sat on one of the stone benches strewn with cushions. The photo lay on the table before her. The young girl stepped forward and said: 'We know this man.'

Mary made a move to get up, but the girl turned to her. 'Madame . . .'

The other women would not look at her. She said again: 'Madame . . .'

Then she lowerd her eyes and said: 'We know where this man is.'

Her eyes were lowered still further: 'He is dead, madame.'

She fell silent and turned. Like the other women, she looked away from Mary, at the ground.

A little later, one of the women got up, picked up the shards of glass and left the courtyard. Not a sound drifted in from without the house. From time to time the old woman shook out her skirts. Her black veil lay across her shoulders, revealing the wiry hair of an old woman tied up in a chignon and pendulous ear-rings. Mary was silent.

When Mariam, the youngest, came towards her she stopped the girl, stood and walked to the far side of the courtyard. All around the yard were the blind eyes of windows curtained in heavy woollen drapes. There was no sound except for the intermittent buzzing of a fly. Mary leaned against the wall. She didn't hear the fly. Tragedy had bided its time; now the words had been spoken and they had torn everything to pieces. Mary didn't feel the hot stone against her back; she searched for something in her which recognised this searing pain, but she found nothing. She pressed her forehead against the stone and the silence about her seemed to grow; she looked around and saw that the women were waiting.

When the old woman came to tell Nour al-Injar al-Koutoubi, she hurried to the courtyard, and as she entered she saw Mary Miller, head down, gripping her glass and she stopped. A ray of sunlight danced on her cheek; Nour al-Koutoubi looked at the women waiting and she closed her eyes. She could see again the eyes of the dead man in the desert. She remembered his gesture that last evening she had seen him, his arms folded against his body, searching to hug something to himself. She walked towards the woman and Mariam explained to Mary who she was. Mary stood and came to her. Nour al-Koutoubi smelled of sweet musk and her skin was sun-scorched.

When she left, an hour later, Mary Miller knew how the women had found the body, why Nour had gone there, alone that first evening, how John had turned to her and spoken, and what her ageing Aunt Nejma had told her on her return; she had heard what John had said in the nights that followed, what he had seen, of the gentleness of his voice and of how she was constantly in his thoughts. Mary asked Nour al-Koutoubi why John had died, but the woman didn't know.

Robert Nantua was not at the place where they had arranged to meet. Mariam and Nour al-Koutoubi suggested that they wait in the gardens by the offices. Women passing in the street stopped to greet them and Nour told them who Mary was. The memory of the body stretched on the dune was suddenly fresh again and the women came to Mary, some of them embraced her, but not one asked anything of her; when Robert pulled up in the jeep she was surrounded by women.

The women watched Mary go, alone, to meet him. She took the first few hesitant steps and stopped. Robert was sure that she would fall; instinctively he stretched out his arms but she flinched and stepped back. Without looking at him, she said: 'He's dead.' Her voice was too low for him to hear and Robert had to ask her to repeat it; her voice, softer still, said it again.

Robert looked at her, and at the women standing silently

around her, and said: 'I know, some of the men told me.' Then he told her that the men were ready to take them to the body and Mary said simply, 'Let's go.'

Ali ben Fakr was there and Robert explained to Mary who he was; two of the men who had gone with him to the dune that first day were there too. Mary asked the women to come with them.

When they left the village the light was beginning to fade. Ali ben Fakr was driving. Sitting in the back of the jeep, Mary watched the procession of dunes veiled red in the coming sunset and she thought that this place had none of the solidity of earth, it was barely substantial, telling men nothing of themselves or of their passing. For the first time she imagined John's body, lying dead in the sand.

They parked the jeep at the bottom of a small dune. Ali ben Fakr turned to speak to Mary, but thought better of it. For a moment all was still and silent, then Robert got down. Mary looked and saw that there was nothing but sand and some clumps of coarse grass.

Ali ben Fakr and the women stood silently, looking towards the dune, then they set off. Ali walked ahead, the women following behind. They knew where they were going. The other men waited by the cars.

Half bent against the wind which had whipped up, Mary found it hard to walk. Her shoes sank into the sand. She looked at Ali ben Fakr walking ahead of her, never stopping, never glancing back, his djellaba and the veils of the women whipping in the wind, their shadows thrown down. She looked at the dunes, the sky, the light. She looked at the women in black, strangers to her, soundlessly climbing the dune ahead, at the French officer in uniform at her side and she stopped. She turned and saw that behind her there was nothing, so she turned again towards them. They were unstoppable, these shadows of strangers walking ever on, never looking back. They had seen John's body in this shapeless desert, had crouched over him, and now they were going back to the place where they had left him without a thought for her. They did not stop and wait for her; they did not know her, did not know she had a dog, had never seen the streets in Provo; they did not even know Provo existed, they simply went on walking. Mary called to Robert Nantua. He turned and walked towards her, stopped. Farther off, he saw Ali ben Fakr, close to the top of the dune, and he knew why she had called him; he called to Ali not to move and hurried on. Mary watched as the two men walked together towards the summit; Ali's arm stretched out, pointing Robert to a place on the horizon, then the two men walked back to meet her.

Robert showed Mary the direction she should take. He told her she would know the place; it was marked with two white stones laid side by side; then he left her.

The veil of dust drawn by the wind from the dunes was thicker now. Mary tightened the scarf around her face as she reached the top of the first dune. On the other side, dunes rose and fell before her and she thought of what they had said about John. She imagined him walking alone on the slope ahead of her and wondered why he had come so far. She drew the veil up to her eyes. She didn't realise that Robert, Ali and the women were following behind, though they were only yards from her.

Mary started down the second slope. She saw the valley that Robert had pointed out to her and, beside it, a flat space. She walked more slowly and saw, from afar, the two stones. She looked at the short distance she still had to cross; looked around and saw there was nothing here; she began to walk again, more slowly still, then she stopped.

The stones had been half covered by the sand. Around them, everything was smooth, untouched, and Mary stared at the missing signs that anyone had passed here. She bowed her head, her knees gave and she knelt on the ground. John's body was here. She bowed further, as though she were falling; her body rocked back and forth as though she were singing, her arms were folded across her stomach; sand drifted on her kneeling form as on a statue; there was no sound but the wind sliding across the dunes; the sky veered towards red; she stayed, her hands pressed against the sand, no heart, as if her heart itself had run away from all of this, no tears; a human thing blown about by the wind; deaf to the sounds of those approaching; unable even to comprehend that they might still exist.

The women were only yards away; motionless, they watched her. Mariam, the youngest, wanted to go to her, but Nour al-Koutoubi held her back. An image of the dead soldier woke in Ali ben Fakr's memory, as it had in the women; death washed over them once more bringing sorrow in its wake.

After a time a woman's voice made Mary turn round; she saw them standing close by, stood up, prepared to run but stopped herself. She gripped John's photo in her hand.

For a moment they formed a tableau. They, waiting, then Mary moved towards the women, looked into their faces and turned; her knees buckled, her shoulders crumpled and they heard her scream, inhuman. Robert felt a sudden surge of feeling for this woman, a feeling like nothing he had ever felt, though he did not yet recognise it. He took a step towards her, his face, laid bare as the wind whipped back his scarf, was more desolate than any soldier going over the top knowing he would not come back. He went to her and the women followed; alone, they knew, Mary would not find it in her to come back to them, words were not enough, she needed now to remember life and who but they could bring it back to her?

Nour al-Koutoubi brushed Robert aside and held Mary to her, speaking to her softly in her own tongue, what matter that the language meant nothing to Mary. Mary did not cry. Nour al-Koutoubi could not feel the weight of the woman's body against her own and so she began to sing, a song her women sang softly when they needed to forget hurtful words, a painful separation, a memory. When at last she felt the weight of Mary's body against her own, she lifted her up and helped her to turn and begin the long walk back. Mariam Manrab, Ali ben Fakr and Robert Nantua walked silently beside them; together they formed a human wall.

Night was falling by the time they got back to the jeep. Ali ben Fakr suggested they spend the night in Rijna and Robert translated his offer. Mary looked at the dunes, the cars, the silent, waiting men and the women. Seeing her hesitate, Nour al-Injar al-Koutoubi went to her, and taking a package from beneath her veil gave it to Mary. Mary turned to Robert then and asked if they could leave.

*

She waited until she was alone in her hotel room before opening the letters. Letters John had given to Nour al-Koutoubi that last night, out of sight of the other women. His last, written the night before the cease-fire, was only a few lines long; she read and reread the final sentence: '. . . Don't worry, hon, it's just like the walks we used to take around the lake. I wish you were here so you could come along. I love you. John.' She laid the letter on the bed. The phone rang. She got up, letting it ring then she crumpled and fell on her knees against the blue serge armchair, where she slept.

When she woke, an hour later, Mary thought she heard a knock at the door, but there was no one there. Her sandals lay at the foot of the bed, her handbag spilled out on to the carpet, John's letters spread across the floor. She wanted someone to come in and pick her up. From the open window she could hear men's voices drifting from the tables around the pool. She wanted them to call to her, to go and sit among them, she wanted to pick up the blue serge armchair and hurl it across the room.

When the phone rang again she hesitated. She looked around her: nothing. She picked up the receiver. The operator asked her to hold. For a moment she thought she heard John's voice, then Robert spoke: he was worried, he had been phoning her room, he wanted to take her to dinner in town. Mary listened to his voice and said nothing. He told her to wait where she was and hung up.

Mary left the receiver humming in the void, she picked up the letters, put them away and went to run a bath. She looked at the clothes lying on the floor and resolved to throw them away the next day. In the bathroom mirror she caught sight of her face and stopped. She thought of John and felt a sharp pain just above her groin, and she looked away. The bath was almost overflowing. She opened the bathroom window a little and slipped into the water.

She wasn't ready when Robert tapped on her door. She put on a dressing-gown, gathered up her clothes and her bag and opened the door. He looked at her but said nothing. She moved aside to let him in, apologising for the mess. Hair wet, arms loaded with her belongings, she said she thought she would like a whisky. Looking at her, Robert was reminded of villages deserted in war; shutters banging, doors open on to empty rooms, everything abandoned in the hurry to get away. He went to her and took her things from her out-stretched arms; the gap in her dressing-gown revealed her skin; she stood, motionless, staring at him. There was noth-ing he could fathom in that look, but he came closer. Her dressing-gown was damp. Her body trembled. He thought she was crying and moved away.

They had dinner in a restaurant on the coast where the ambassador had taken them the first evening. Afterwards they walked along the beach. Rolls of barbed wire criss-crossed the sand, signalling the position of mines. The air was acrid with the smell of burning oil. Neither of them spoke of what they might do in the days to come.

Later, Robert took Mary back to the hotel. She walked ahead of him down the empty corridor. She stood tall in a simple tunic and cotton trousers, her head down, her hair swept up to reveal the nape of her neck. Her handbag hung on her arm. A dozen times he thought she would fall, a dozen times he reached out to catch her, each time in vain. Then she stopped, took off her sandals and walked on without looking round. Not for the first time, he could feel his desire for her: her back to him, her shoulders shaking sometimes, trembling.

She opened the door to her room and went in. She didn't close it behind her, but walked towards the window. Robert followed her and stood there in the middle of the room. He watched as she opened the drawer of the bedside table and took out the envelope which Nour al-Koutoubi had given her; she took out a letter and handed it to him, then sat on the window-sill and untied her hair. Robert sat on the blue serge armchair and read the letter. He put it down and thought about the war, then he turned to her. She was watching him. The room was lit by the floodlights on the hotel. He went over to her and put his hands on her neck, but she dropped her head quickly and he pulled his hands away. He thought about John Miller, about this death that he knew nothing about and said: 'I'll find out why your husband died.'

She turned to him. 'I don't want his body exhumed.'

'Don't you want to know?'

'Know what?'

'Why he died?'

'I know already.'

'The letter . . . you think he killed himself?'

'No, I don't.'

'So, what?'

'So do whatever you have to, but leave his body there; he died there.'

She picked up the bottle of whisky and poured herself a

glass; muffled music drifted up from the hotel night-club several floors below. Neither of them spoke, each gauging the loneliness, the tiredness that had overcome them. Robert thought again about John and about his own life. He thought about the barracks, about his wife, his sons and about going home; he felt a sharp pain in his chest. He asked Mary for a drink and sat down again. Below, the music from the night-club stopped. They heard a woman's laugh from the room next door. Mary clasped her hands together. Robert watched her; his life fell around him like shed skin. She had dug it out without knowing it and thrown it as a child throws a frisbee; now it hung in the air, spinning, frantic, making a high-pitched hum, trying to move. He put down the whisky glass, got up and said good-night to Mary Miller.

When he got to the door he turned and told her that if she needed any help filling out the forms he would be happy to oblige, and left, unsure whether she had replied. Back in his room there was a message from his wife; he went to bed.

In the middle of the night, when Mary knocked on his door, Robert moved in his sleep, as though pulling something to him. He opened the door and saw her there, her dressing-gown floating against her body, her hair down, and for a second he didn't recognise her. She held out her hand towards him in silent apology and he squeezed it and let it drop. The image of a girl, an Algerian girl lying naked, dead outside her village flashed through his mind; he wanted to tell Mary to leave, but she was already inside.

*

The only light in the room is from a lamp in the hallway. He can hear her move to the window and stop. He imagines her leaning against the frame; he turns; she is looking at him.

She looks beautiful and he tells her so, but she doesn't hear. And then his hands move to the nape of her neck   his fingers slip through her hair   his mouth trembles before finding hers   his body presses against hers   his hands are burning as they move over her   brush her warm shoulders, the hollow of her throat   disappear between her breasts and on to her soft belly which is wet as her lips in which his own lips lose themselves   her body welded to his they walk to the unmade bed   he feels her fold into him   he arches against her body   she turns towards him, her dressing-gown open   her body revealed   she waits for him to come to her   his shoulders blotting out her shoulders his belly, his thighs blotting out her belly, her thighs   his body covers hers   he closes his eyes   he can hear her breathing   he doesn't move   he sees her   she encompasses everything   she lifts him up hurls him far away and he is lost   she does this without a move   what she is is enough   he has nothing to hold on to for the first time   his body slides over hers   he grips her neck   her lips   he holds her, holds   he holds her body, hard as an angel sculpted in stone, never letting go   his lips pressed low make his face seem part of her body   he lifts his body   slides his penis, which no longer seems a part of him, into the dark body of this woman and finds there an infinite softness that lifts him so high and hard that his body shudders with a cry and breaks that last veil that separates him from her and is surprised by desire like he has never felt before letting go and feeling their bodies wrapped together   giving them life   he looks at Mary   he dares to look into her face which makes no choice not knowing if he will live   and his eyes are not afraid to stay on her face   he loves her and tells her so   he is not waiting for a response and that makes him love her more.

A knot of pain in Mary melted away; she knew what this man had to lose; she knew that he had nothing left; she had seen his desire, his arms reaching out thinking he could catch her should she fall, when all he wanted was to hold her; he had requested nothing, had not asked the foolish questions that keep death company; and so she let his flesh find its place in hers; she knew what peace, what defeat was waiting for him, and when he took her to him again, made love to her again, she closed her eyes, she opened her arms and she allowed this man, this stranger, to bring her a muted pleasure, alien and unknown.

The slept side by side, barely touching. At dawn she woke and lay there, her eyes open. She was thinking of John.

As she felt day break, Mary got up. Robert woke and looked at her. He called to her. She answered without turning from the window where she watched the sun rise.

Later, they went back to the dunes. Mary wanted to see the people of Rijna once more. The women welcomed her with such gentleness that she wanted to remain. They stayed for two days and two nights. Then they made their way back and went their separate ways. Robert Nantua still had work to do. Mary Miller's work was done.

8

somewhere in a desert (iii)

epilogue

No one knew when the war had started; perhaps it had been a long time ago, maybe it was there since the beginning. Those who searched for reasons, for the whys and wherefores, did so because they wanted to believe that there had been a time before the war and that there would come a time when it would end. But they were wrong. War came out of desire; it was part of the memory of children, it was born before them and would shadow them, the sons like their fathers, and it would live on after them.

When they felt it close in they tried to shout it down, to fend it off with voices of reason; they felt every sinew retracting; the blood coursing in their veins, hurtling through them as though it could escape, but hardly did the embers spark to flame once more but they were drawn inexorably towards it. When it abated they could feel its absence weighing on them.

They did not know when the war had begun, nor what name to give it, what place to make for it in their lives, though they knew it as they knew their oldest friends. What they did not know was peace. There was no peace, since the war had not ended. That which they called peace they did in error, it was simply the absence of war. Peace itself was something quite different. It would tax their imagination even to conceive what it might be, such imagination being at odds with who they were.

For two days and two nights John Miller had walked across the dunes, little knowing the war had ended, when at sunset he stopped. He felt an unexpected desire for peace, a sudden hope that, though he did not know it, was born out of the war itself. He sat on the sand and tried to understand this feeling surging in him like love.

A bloody twilight settled around him part gold, part fire; high overhead a vulture circled, head back, wings outstretched. He stared into the firestorm sky and watched the bird. It made no sound. It danced on the air, solitary, its flight shifting between great swoops to earth and long, measured glides. It seemed intent only on its tireless flight. Shooting across the sky like a skater speeding across the ice, it raised its huge wings and beat them once, twice, in great arcs the better to glide. The laws of physics seemed alien to it, vaulting into heaven, its flight made gravity seem like the childish fear of dwarves and timorous dogs. The bird itself carved out the laws of physics, toying with them in its flight, as though all that mattered was the beauty of motion. The air rushed to meet the beating wings, and not the wings the air; it stroked the air, fashioned it as a sculptor models damp clay. Nothing held it back, the bird seemed to possess the sky itself. John watched it for a long time, he climbed the dune to get a better view and laughed the sudden rush of peace he had felt mirrored in the high, solitary dance of this bird, drunk on freedom. He breathed deeply and felt something surge within him, something beyond the war, and for a happy instant he thought that peace was there within his grasp.

He should have returned to M Camp. He had been due to arrive at the command post the night before. His place was there, but he was not. He had gone; had he been in Provo he would have left by the garden gate and walked out towards the lake. But he was not in Provo and there was no lake, no yellow buses, no motels peppering the roadside; there was no road.

He had crossed the border, leaving his things in an old, deserted border post: four walls eaten away by the wind, the door frames missing. He left the jeep and carried on on foot, taking only a compass, his water flask, a little food and some paper.

He quickly abandoned the trail left by the tanks rolling to battle in the other direction. He crossed the flat sandy plains that ran along the border and started across the dunes, clambering slowly up the steep slopes to see how far they stretched, before running down the other side. Sometimes he turned, wondering if he would be able to find his way back, before dismissing the thought. He had never felt so much like walking. In the hours that followed it was all that mattered to him.

From time to time he stopped, slept for a few hours, then went on; in the two days he had been walking he had not seen, even from afar, the shadow of another human soul. He liked the heat. He liked the night. He liked the first flush of dawn and the twilight. He looked around him at the beauty as it cycled through day and night, thinking at any moment, at the crest of a dune, it would disappear, but it did not, it was everywhere, blinding in its brightness. He opened his shirt and closed his eyes. He could feel the air about him hum, the sand move almost imperceptibly underfoot, and all before him, uninterrupted, the earth stretched away like a continent and he could imagine himself in a world untouched by human hand. This did not conjure in him any feelings of power: it was a simple, sudden sense of new freedom.

In this vast, teeming world, life seemed to rise up spontaneously, packed close as a fist, heady as spice and yet soft. He had felt it, sensed this promise even as a child. September in the mountains in Vermont. Tom was there, Judith and Bobby. They were ten years old, maybe younger, and he would run through the forests and over the grassy banks into the evening, winding past waterfalls and through glades, his heart already pulsing with secret joy. Other boys still needed their mothers close, but he had a furious passion for life driven by his awakening sense of freedom; the passion of the sprinter, of climbers eyeing the rocky summits, hungry, transfigured. It was this passion which lifted him above the days and months, never thinking to look back. He had forgotten that now. Here in the dunes, running from the war, John felt as though this was his first taste of freedom. And so, after two days' and two nights' walking, he stopped at nightfall, his heart heady with a joy he thought was new to him.

The long miles across the sandy plains and the undulating dunes had driven out anger and fear, the thunder of the tanks, the men's screams; the silence that fell about him reached some dull pain which had festered in him for months, certain of his defeat. Here, lying on the dune, his head thrown back staring into the skies, he felt at last at rest, at peace. If this were Provo, he would have been sitting by the lake, watching the birds fly south, waiting for the night to come. Remembered images of Provo, of the lake, flashed through him and, looking around him at the dunes, he found himself wondering if this relief was not peace, but simply the absence of war. He was surprised by the thought, not quite sure he even understood it. If there was war, then there was peace? Could peace exist without war? How could there be men without man, murderers without murder, victim without wounds? He smiled at these strange thoughts conjured by the desert; he thought of Mary and spoke her name. He thought about the war he had lived through and his life before, of the elms in Central Park and Sundays in Brooklyn stifling in the quiet heat. He thought about moving inside the body of Mary Miller and the love he had felt suddenly bathe him. He remembered the lanes running through New York University, straight as a plumb-line, of the blue suits and wing collars worn by students sitting their bar exams, remembered the squirrels on the rickety park benches in Vermont. He thought of his mother. Of his father. Of the sign hanging on the garage door. Of the high whistle of the subway from the kitchen window. Of the Commodore cinema. Of himself, somewhere in a desert. He said his name aloud, John Paul Miller, his full name. There was no echo. He lay down, then, and slept.

A dream woke him, a dream reproducing in almost every detail an incident at B Camp three days before. The 112th were stationed there. The land offensive was well under way. The night before two sections had opened up a route for the tanks through the dunes, into enemy territory. Two kids from Provo who had been on the mission told him about it. Driving the route through, they drove slap bang into an enemy battalion holed up in a trench in the dunes. There they were, with a fleet of bulldozers, faced with an enemy they had not expected. They would have to round up the prisoners of war before they could make headway. 'They told us there wasn't time,' Morrison said, looking away from John. 'We just went on ahead.' They hadn't even stopped. They had driven their bulldozers over the men and buried them alive, the mechanical shovels filling the trenches. They had their orders.

John stared into their childish faces; Morrison, Neuman and Valentin, then went to Stewart's tent. In his monotone drawl the commander said that he was cut up about having to make the decision, but the men, the trenches, were slowing their advance, what the hell could he do with all those prisoners? He looked at John and said, 'What the hell's the matter with you?' but John didn't answer.

The following morning he was sent on to make contact

with M Camp. He drove for a long time, then stopped. Here there was nothing but sand and sky. He got down from the jeep and sat, looking at his map; got in again and turned back. He headed due south, towards the border.

The vulture had disappeared. The fire on the horizon guttered in dark purples and golds, the air was cooler; for the first time since he had left, John felt alone. The dream that had woken him had swept away his feeling of peace. He looked at the dunes, wondering if he had not come further than he thought, whether he would be able to go back. The sky was empty. He stared at the desert, unmarked by the smallest human trace. He felt cold: scared, suddenly, as frightened as the kid he had been thirty years ago standing on a street corner in Brooklyn.

His mother had sent him out to get milk from a shop two streets away. It was a rainy morning in September. John, sliding along the wet kerbstones, one foot on the road, the other on the kerb, straddling the river in the gutter, had completely forgotten the money in his hand, the milk his mother had sent him to buy. He came to a crossroads where the kerb ended; people hurried past huddled in their raincoats, suddenly he didn't know where he was any more. He couldn't see the El, he looked around desperately to find the synagogue, the cinema, the shop where he was headed. He felt terrified and stood there for a long time, unable to move, not knowing what to do, how to budge. Eventually a man came up to him and, after asking everyone who passed if they knew the boy, walked him to his home two streets away.

He could not remember that fear, only the man who had walked him home, or perhaps his mother knew the story. He could not recollect the day when he stopped on the pavement because all at once he did not know where he was going, or why. It was the same fear that gripped him now none the less, a fear that was alien to him.

He scanned the sky for a bird, but there were none, or a tree, but there were no trees either. He sat down and a thought flickered across his mind that he might die here. Maybe he had come too far. Perhaps he would never find his way back and no one would think to search for him here. He closed his eyes and wondered whether anyone realised he was missing. He buried his fist in the sand and turned over, open-mouthed against the dune. His face pressed against the sand, his desert boots, his regimental number 59–367, he laughed and thought: 'I'm like a dog. I just need a lamp-post to piss on.' He didn't see the figure coming towards him. It was far off still and hidden by the dune.

He took a sheet of paper and wrote:

Honey. I've crossed the border and am fifty degrees west, somewhere in a desert. I needed to get away. Needed a walk. Don't worry, just out walking. Threw away my dog tags – 59–367 – dumped everything else in an old border post. Maybe I've deserted. I love you, I need you here. I need to know if you still love me just a little. I didn't want things to turn out this way. Didn't know what else to do. Why did you fall in love with me? Tell me why. I'm going to walk a bit more, then I'll go back. Don't worry. I love you. John.

He folded the paper and put it in his shirt pocket, then he stretched out on the sand and stayed there for a long time, blood hammering in his heart, watching the sky and letting the silence fall around him again. The sand rustled on the dunes and the air was soft, humid, like a late summer evening. He closed his eyes and thought about peace. It was something more than the absence of war, but he didn't quite know what it was. Then, again, he fell asleep.

When he woke he was thinking of Mary. He had been dreaming of her, sitting here on the sand beside him, her hand on his belly. He turned on his side, as though he held her in his arms, imagined her body pressed against his own, her hands, her laugh, she lay facing him, smiling and he hugged the empty space between his arms tighter and thought he would cry. He stood up and looked at the dune, at the imprint of his body in the sand, and remembered that minutes ago he had thought he might die in this place. He felt ashamed somehow that he had considered stopping here for no reason; as if sitting here, giving up, were enough to kill him. He wanted to turn and head back; he had come far, but he knew he had it in him to face the long walk back and the inevitable questions. Once he was there, he would know what to do. This was not peace, only the absence of war, he knew that, but it didn't matter, perhaps it had always been so.

He brushed the sand from his clothes. He stretched, stared one last time into the empty sky overhead. He didn't hear the click sound behind him.

It took some seconds before he realised he was not alone. He made to turn, thinking he had been found, when a voice told him not to move.

*

He stops short. Hears the rustle of clothes, then nothing. The silence lasts a moment. He stands facing the copper sky, his arms held away from his body. He waits. Then he hears footsteps coming towards him across the sand and feels someone standing behind him. He feels his muscles tense. His mind is empty. Something presses into his back, something cold which slides along his skin to his left shoulder-blade, then stops. He knows it is a gun barrel.

Sweat trickles on his forehead. The sun, directly ahead, flashes blindingly on the sand. He starts to speak. He says he is not armed, that he would like to turn round so that the man can see him, then he waits. The man says nothing, but he senses the pistol withdrawing. He feels his muscles relax. He thinks he should turn round, but is wary of making any sudden movements. For several seconds everything is quiet again. John waits on the dune, silent, watching the sky darken. The bird has not come back. There is a crack of gunfire.

John feels the bullet enter his back, just below the shoulder-blade, even as he hears the shot. The pain is immediate, but brief, like a burn. The bullet rips through his flesh, then tears the bone. John's heart tightens. Slowed by the mass of body, the bullet comes to a stop in the right ventricle of his heart. It seems to waver. Around it the heart beats, the arteries pulse, then it spins suddenly. His flesh retracts, opens, then the bullet explodes. It was designed to do so in contact with flesh.

A shockwave pulses through John's body. He feels bathed in a sudden wave of heat. His heart is torn apart, his body contracts around it. There is something like a struggle as his muscles tense and his limbs splay as if to try and hold himself together, but blood erupts from the wound and spatters the ground. Now John feels the pain rush through him, compact but diffuse, bending his body double; exploding at the base of his neck, it is like nothing he has ever felt. His penis hardens. He lifts his head. He feels his body tense as though shaken with violent passion. A moment later he feels nothing and falls back.

The blind man's son stands behind him, holding his rifle. He waits for John to fall before taking the three steps that separate them. He wonders if John is dead. This is the first time he has killed, but he feels nothing unusual, he is not relieved, not happy. As John's body hits the ground he moves forward and leans over him, curious to see the face of the man he has just killed, but he sees nothing, as though he were looking through a shard of glass.

Through a haze, John looks at the blind man's son leaning over him. He sees the hunting rifle the boy is holding. He feels a grimace distort his face, he is trying to speak, but no words come.

The boy leans still, his face so close that John can feel his breath. He sees the wide eyes, knows they are searching to find out what death is like, but knows too that they see nothing. Nobody has ever looked at him with this empty stare; the boy's eyes seem to be looking for something but not at him, they cannot see him, cannot see anything. John knows now that he will not say anything. He need only look. Though he does not know why, he knows this man will wait for him to die here.

John strains to keep his eyes open. He watches the blind

man's son carefully. He sees an ancient fear on the boy's face and thinks it has always been there, that it is this fear which has made the face angular, shifty with a flicker of madness in his eyes. There is something else in this face, the remnants of peace long sought after, a search that was always deferred, always abandoned; it is there in a softness of the brow, in the cheeks, he wants to reach out and stroke them. He tries to reach out his hand, but it does not answer and lies stiffly on the sand.

The sky above them blackens. John is cold. He feels a great tiredness run through his body. He does not want to look at this man leaning over him, haggard, unable to speak. He wants him to leave. He wants to tell him to go, but has no strength to speak. He turns his face away. He can barely see the sky, wavering between fire and shadow. He can feel the heat of the man as he leans over. He knows he cannot keep his eyes open much longer and closes them a moment to rest. The blind man's son wonders if he is dead, reaches out and shakes him, but John opens his eyes again and hears the man murmur. He cannot understand what the other is saying, but he knows the sound – it reminds him of an old man's threats muttered between clenched teeth to John every day as he passed on his way to school. This is the same sound: deep, tremulous, heavy with blame.

John turns back to the blind man's son and smiles at him. For a moment he does not react, his pupils dilating a little perhaps, and John sees in them a new fear; his smile broadens and marshalling what strength he has left, he parts his lips and says 'salaam (peace)'. The blind man's son stands up and looks elsewhere.

The man with the rifle is turned away from him now, his shoulders clenched. John knows he will leave. He watches him grip his gun, a trickle of sweat on the nape of his neck, sand sticking to his djellaba. His back is slender, like a boy's, making him look somehow unfinished. He stands, motionless, on the dune. John wonders what he is waiting for. He sees him turn towards him, stare at his body, thinks perhaps he will finish him off, but he looks up and stares into the sky, then turns again and walks away.

John waited until the blind man's son disappeared. He stretched his arms and legs, felt the sand beneath his head, beneath his body. He felt no pain. His life ebbed out, like a dog on the roadside. He was surprised to find that his body did not fight, he felt no need to move, to scream, to sob; simply that he might sleep. It was a gentle sensation, something he might feel after a day spent at the beach.

The sky was black above him now. He held off closing his eyes for a long time, but his body was drained of strength, of blood; he let his eyelids fall.

It was death that made him open his eyes again. He had felt a cold breeze pass over him, so icy it was as though he had never been warm. He felt dazed, a sudden empty feeling like death. He tried to lift his head but it lay heavily on the sand. He thought he could see the bird again, gliding in slow circles above him as he died, but the sky was empty. Nothing stirred. Silence fell over everything, pronouncing that night had

come. He felt afraid, a nameless, boundless fear, a sudden will to be saved, for someone to come and lift him, cradle him and stand him again on the earth, someone to say, its over, it's all over. He tried to open his lips, but they remained closed. He tried to sit up, to turn round; he tried to reach out, to open his eyes, but it was useless. He felt his stomach heave, a bitter taste flooded his mouth and he experienced a sharp, terrible pang of regret. For the last time he tried to open his eyes and he saw the sky, black as a pit. Furious colours raged in him and he felt his whole body lifted. Then it fell back, hard and stiff as cold steel. He was barely breathing. He felt death was almost here, *was* here. He was afraid once more; like a mongrel dying by the roadside with no one to see him, or speak to him. He felt a profound sense of loathing. He had run away from war, from killing, from those who killed; he thought he could stand aside, assert that he was not like them. He might just as well assert that he was not like men; in killing him, the blind man's son had brought back to him what he was. Tears trickled on his cheeks. He wanted to get up, to leave, to go back to where he belonged. But in this, too, he was wrong. He was dying, he would not get up again, this was where he belonged.

John Miller cried for a time, his tears wearing fine wrinkles in his cheeks. He was aware of their warmth, a last warmth he was surprised to feel still. He remembered the softness of rain falling on him, of diving into the warm waters of the south seas, and the memory calmed him. His breath took up again, slow and shallow. The fear had gone, leaving a grain of peace, the gentle peace of truce. From it came his last thought, the final image of all men in their last hour. He saw life stand

before him, something distinct, something other than his flesh; it cried, as if in pain, then stood and raised itself to its full height. It stood like a blade, so tall and straight, as though it had cut its ties with all that is human. John focused his last conscious thought on it and watched, thinking it must break. How could it stand so still, so strong, careless of death, but it raised itself higher. He could see it, rising before him, criss-crossed with old scars and bruises, and a hard, perfect beauty. He saw it, arced like the vault of a cathedral, strong and glassy like the marble that gives each Madonna and her child their dignity, the curve of their cheeks. A moment later and it seemed smooth as a grain of barley. Not moving, not smiling, it simply was, like a child waiting to be born, and John Miller loved it with a force he never thought possible; every sinew of the body which had carried him thus far opened to it. A smile spread on his dry lips and life gave him a taste of the rain that swells the dry earth, of sun melting a highway, of the smell of leather, of paper in a freshly printed book, of bacon frying, of the light of evening in summer and the black, black colour of Mary Miller's skin. It showed him the withered hand with its antique wedding band, the baby incapable of knowing the life that will one day grow in her and suckle the breast she does not yet have, it lets him hear the murmur of old women, their skin wrinkled and soft, sitting on their stoop, and the song, mysterious and clear, of men in love, the dull sound of children's drums played at a parade and the high, regal voice of Jessye Norman. The sound of water under a ship's hull. Light glittering in Mary Miller's eyes. The rusted garage door. His mother's name. And his own, which was his father's also.

And then it laughed a small laugh like a child's, and tears fell again on John Miller's face. One last time, he sensed himself rise up to his full height to see again the vastness of life. Then he felt himself weak, shadowy, and knew that soon all would be still. There was a sudden clamour inside him, a pain, and he did not know if it was life or death thrashing there. For the last time he wanted to know life, to remember and to hold the thought of it. He tried to move towards it, to look at it; it stood there, pale, looking gently on him, but already it was farther off, already they were parting.

John Miller's heart skipped. His body shuddered once, twice; he felt the pain again; he could see nothing now. He felt the pain inside his head, soon he could feel nothing else; he embraced it, flowed with it and came at last to the heart of this inhuman suffering. He looked at life and saw it, barely a wisp, no thicker than a paper handkerchief, it was far off now, almost outside him, like a veil, a scrap of paper in the wind, a white pebble. Still John Miller stared as though he would imprint it on his memory. He wanted to feel it weigh on him again, but he could not, it was far off. The pain eased a little. His heart was barely beating now. He saw life struggle, surrender with a whimper, then it was gone. It seemed to him he saw it arch; soon it was merely a form, blurred and indistinct. John Miller's body shuddered again and life disappeared into air.

Alone, John Miller remembered the men he had known, the faces of women, of old men and children he had met, eyes turned towards the sea or to some dry riverbed. He thought about who they were and what they wished to be, all the while feeling the coldness creep over him. He was surprised that he could feel it still and died shortly after, his last thought: part regret that he had not the strength to walk farther; part longing to live everything over; pain that this longing had not come sooner and amazement that it should end like this.